High Desert Barbecue

A Tale of Suspense, Pyromania and Sexual Tension

by J.D. Tuccille

High Desert Barbecue

This is a work of fiction. All the characters and events portrayed in this book are fictional, and any resemblance to real people or incidents is purely coincidental.

Stubbed Toe Press
Cornville, Arizona

ISBN-13: 978-1466448308
ISBN-10: 146644830X

Photo Credits:
Cover photo: Bureau of Land Management/California

*For Wendy, who had no idea what she was
in for when she married a writer.*

A note to my readers:

You know this, but I'll tell you anyway, since somebody, somewhere, probably didn't get the memo. This is a novel. A work of fiction. The author has played fast and loose with settings, geography and time frames—particularly with regard to Sycamore Canyon—for the purpose of telling an entertaining yarn. Please don't attempt to use this novel as a hiking guide.

Chapter 1

Rollo sat under the cover of the Ponderosa pines framing a steep ridge line, gnawing a piece of venison jerky and washing it down with sips of warm water from a dusty, fabric-covered canteen. He watched the Forest Service workers below. He watched them warily, back in the shade of the trees where he was lost in shadow beneath the wind-bent branches. Rollo didn't get along well with the khaki-shirted federal employees. Forest Service personnel had but recently destroyed his house, stolen his truck and sent him fleeing into the forest.

Of course, Rollo's house was a hand-built shack on federal land and his truck was an unregistered beater he'd salvaged from a dump. But he'd really liked that little shack, what with its views off Arizona's Mogollon Rim to Sycamore Canyon below and its mostly waterproof roof to fend off the monsoon rains, rare though they were during drought years. The shack he could build again—he'd done it before. But the truck was a real loss. Now he'd have to hoof it into town for supplies and to visit his friends. Williams was a long walk with a full pack, and Flagstaff was out of the question until he had new wheels.

Such is the life of a modern mountain man. Or social dropout. Or loser. Rollo's ex-wife definitely would have gone with

~1~

"loser." But, then again, thought Rollo, Toni hated the outdoors and couldn't build a campfire for shit.

Rising on slightly creaky knees—45 was just around the corner and Rollo hadn't had time to properly stretch before donning his heavy backpack and sprinting (well, lurching) from the marauding rangers—he finished his water, capped the canteen, and looked around.

That's when he noticed the Forest Service Chevy Blazer parked at the mouth of a dry wash, out-of-sight of the cluster of workers clearing the debris that had recently been his hovel-with-a-view.

"I'll betcha … I'll just betcha those dumbasses left the keys in the ignition," Rollo muttered out loud.

He started walking, slowly but eagerly, through the brush, descending to the wash and the concealed Blazer. The high, dry grass rustled as he passed, and pine cones crunched softly underfoot. Within a few minutes, he stood by the open window of the Blazer, and let out a low whoop—audible only to him and to a curious prairie dog watching from the edge of its hidey hole.

"It's only fair," Rollo said to himself as he tossed his pack across the cab into the shotgun seat, slipped behind the wheel and took hold of the key. "They took my truck. Now I take theirs."

He paused and glanced back in the direction of the hidden Forest Service workers. He snorted, loudly. Then he shifted the Blazer into neutral, released the emergency brake, stepped out, and began pushing against the open driver's door. The truck barely budged, then eased, slowly, onto the jeep road that had brought it to this spot. Silently, Rollo guided the truck around a bend and down a flat stretch of road.

Glancing over his shoulder, the straining man saw a thin column of smoke rise into the sky.

"Bastards can't just wreck my house; they have to burn it,

too," he grumbled. Then he hopped behind the wheel and started the engine. For a few minutes he kept his speed down to minimize dust and engine noise. Then, as his old homesite shrank in the rearview mirror, he jammed on the accelerator and sped his new vehicle down the dirt road in the direction of the Interstate. A high column of dust kicked up behind, mingling with the smoky haze gathering in the air.

Rollo howled with laughter.

An hour later, the Forest Service truck sat in the driveway of a small house on the north side of Flagstaff. Rollo forced the flimsy latch on the back door, leaving a small spray of splinters projecting from the doorframe, grabbed a cold beer from the refrigerator, and planted himself on the sofa.

Which is where the homeowner found him upon returning from the market.

Chapter 2

When Scott entered his house through his front door—his unlocked front door—he saw a stocky, middle-aged man on his sofa. The man had long salt-and-pepper hair tucked under a wide-brimmed canvas hat, and wore a ratty plaid shirt with greasy corduroy shorts. A pair of heavy hiking boots rested on the floor, the feet they'd formerly confined stretched across the coffee table.

The room smelled strongly of unwashed ... well ... *everything*.

"The least you could do is open a window, Rollo."

"I'm on the lam, Scott. I didn't want to draw attention to myself."

Scott crossed the living room, passing through the archway into the kitchen where he deposited the plastic shopping bag from the supermarket on the counter. Then he helped himself to a beer from the refrigerator.

"On the lam? Does anybody even say that anymore?"

The back door into the kitchen hung slightly open. Scott poked at the spray of splinters probing into the room.

"Hey, you know the front door was unlocked, right?"

"Unlocked? Shit." A muffled shuffling noise, like that of greasy fabric rubbing against upholstery, came from the living room. "Sorry. I'll fix that lock."

"Anyway," Scott said, returning to the living room "if you wanted to keep a low profile, you probably shouldn't have parked the Forest Service truck in my driveway."

"Too obvious, is it?"

"Just a bit."

Scott perched himself on the lodge-pole pine sofa arm at the opposite end from Rollo. He fanned his hand at the older man.

Rollo pointedly looked away, and took another long sip of beer.

"That truck, Rollo. Is that something I'm likely to have to explain to anybody who sees it parked by my house?"

Rollo shrugged.

"Well, move it then."

"OK."

Scott took a deep breath, and then wrinkled his nose at his mistake.

"All right, I'll bite. Why are you on the lam?"

"Those khaki-shirted bastards burned my house and stole my truck."

Scott squinted.

"Are you talking about that shack of yours and the rolling deathtrap you got from the junkyard?"

"That's an unkind way of putting it. Anyway, I'm without a house at the moment, though I have new wheels."

"That would be the Forest Service truck."

Rollo brandished an index finger, wagging it back and forth so rapidly it seemed to have no bones. "Hey, they owe me a vehicle."

"It hardly seems a fair trade, seeing as how this truck has functioning brakes and the like." Scott shook his head. "Anyway, what do you mean they burned your house?"

"I saw it burning as I made my getaway." Rollo paused. "At least, I think they did. They tore my house down and I saw smoke rising from the spot where the rangers were vandalizing my stuff."

"Huh. That's the place overlooking Sycamore Canyon, right?"

"Yep, the same one you saw on your last visit."

"That's a hell of a place to set a fire. It's full of brush and the place is bone dry—it will be until we get some decent rain."

Rollo snorted. "Rangers are a bunch of dipshits. They don't know from dry."

Scott nodded. While they were a mixed bunch, he'd met some boneheads in the local Forest Service ranks, and he could think of a few who made Rollo look like a paragon of sensible life choices.

"So you came here because ..."

"Any chance I can stay here tonight?"

Scott closed one eye and pursed his lips.

"Oh come on."

"Yeah, you can stay. But you have to shower and wash your clothes before you touch anything else—and I mean *anything* else. And the truck goes."

"Done."

"And you have to clear out for a while. Lani is coming over and she's not your number-one fan."

Rollo shrugged. Then he rose from the sofa and drained his beer.

"I'll be back later. I have a few chores to run."

"Murphy's raised their beer prices. And that escort service you like got busted."

"Shit." Rollo clenched a fist. "Cities are only good for bars and hookers. What's the point of visiting 'em if they're gonna make it a hassle?"

"You'll figure something out."

"I guess. See ya later."
Rollo walked toward the front door.
"Don't forget to get that truck out of my driveway."

Chapter 3

With Rollo gone, Scott took his half-finished beer down the corridor to the second bedroom, which was outfitted as an office. Without sitting, he flicked his computer mouse with the tip of his finger to get rid of the screen saver. The gesture revealed a long line of new, unread e-mail messages and he groaned. He quickly peeled off his light nylon jacket and short-sleeved, button-down shirt, and kicked off his shoes. That left him wearing denim shorts, sunglasses and a straw cowboy hat.

He opened the first e-mail—and groaned louder than before. "A meeting?"

Then he opened the attached file on a second e-mail and started printing. As the printer spit pages, he double-clicked the media software on his laptop, and started shuffling randomly through its full load of music. Toby Keith's "I'm Just Talkin' About Tonight" filled the room.

When ten pages were stacked in the printer tray, with more on the way, he grabbed the pile of papers, shoved them in the fax machine resting on the file cabinet by the window, punched the button for a pre-set number, and sent an electronic stream of numbers and pie charts flowing through the telephone lines.

The phone rang.

Scott retrieved headphones from under the piles of paper on his desk, all held in place by a Colt Mark IV Series 80 .45-caliber pistol used as a paper weight, and plugged them into the laptop, cutting Toby off in mid-proposition. He donned the headphones under his hat, leaving his right ear uncovered, and then answered the phone.

"Scott here."

"Hey Scott, it's Brian here in the office, with Jennifer, Kathy, Todd and Justin."

"Hey guys!"

He was answered by a round of "heys."

"How's Arizona treating you?"

"Oh, you know how it is. Another lousy day in paradise." Scott danced slowly around the room, more or less in rhythm with the music in his headphones.

"See any moose recently?"

"Elk, Todd. We have elk here. I almost got mugged by one the other day."

Scott shot a glance toward the fax machine, which was slowly digesting the last page in the tray.

"Hey, did you guys get my Web-traffic report?"

"No," Brian answered. "I was going to ask you about that. Did you send it through?"

The fax machine emitted a low buzz as it sent the last bits of data streaming off to New York.

"Yep. If it's not in your hands, it should be sitting on your fax machine. The news is good, by the way. Traffic is up and the new small-business section seems to be a big draw."

"Wait a minute."

Scott recognized Todd's voice.

"Are we really still e-mailing the data off to Scott, to print out and fax back to us?"

The telephone speaker remained silent for a long moment as Scott promenaded across his office to the opening strains of a 1980s-era Pogues song.

"Uh oh," he mouthed to himself.

"Well ... yeah," Brian answered. "The networking site is his baby. Scott is responsible for submitting all the reports for his area of responsibility."

"But that raises another issue," Kathy said.

You bitch, Scott thought. I'm being ambushed.

"What exactly is Scott's area of responsibility?"

"I'm editor of the networking and development site," Scott answered, slowing his fancy footwork so exertion wouldn't show in his voice.

"But what do you edit?" Kathy asked. "Didn't we out-source all of our content something like two years ago?"

"Well ... he does write a column," Brian chimed in. "You write a column, don't you, Scott?"

"Every week!"

"And what about the newsletter?" Brian asked, grasping at a slender straw. Brian was Scott's manager and had signed off on his continued employment through repeated reviews.

"The newsletters are all automated," Todd said. "They even send themselves."

A long pause ensued. Scott resigned himself to the inevitable

"What about managing staff?" The voice sounded like Justin.

"I'll take this one," Scott said, hoping to get the painful process done with. "Nope, we let go of the last of my staff sometime last year. That was Cathleen. Nice girl. We ran out of stuff for her to do."

"Then what is it we're paying you for?"

Scott thought long and hard, keeping his feet in motion to the music as he did so. He banged his shin against a fully loaded backpack perched atop a pile of camping gear that occupied the corner of his office, winced, and then turned his attention back to the conversation.

"Well, aside from the column, you're pretty much paying me to print out e-mails you send me and fax 'em back to you."

Another long pause ensued.

"So, Todd, out of curiosity … What is it that *you* do?"

Chapter 4

Fortunately for Lani's peace of mind, she had no idea that her boyfriend had taken in a lodger. A woman of passionately held beliefs wrapped up in a petite blonde package, Lani passionately believed that Rollo was a lazy bum and at least a low-grade menace to the public good. The fact that the subject of her disdain wouldn't necessarily dispute her description didn't improve her outlook one bit.

She also passionately loved Scott, so she tolerated his itinerant friend—barely.

And she also liked kids. Which was good, since she spent a lot of time with them as a teacher.

"Hey Miss Roche!"

Lani peeled her eyes from the box of feminine pads in her hand. Regular or slender, she pondered. There were so many choices. She looked around for the source of the greeting. Nobody was visible up the aisle of the supermarket, and the large, dark-skinned woman in the other direction was facing away.

"Miss Roche!"

She looked down.

"How's it goin', Miss Roche?"

"Oh, Ozzie. How are you?" She tossed the box—regular it

was—over her shoulder into the shopping cart.

"He's in summer school, Miss Roche." The large woman she'd noticed before wheeled a cart that groaned under its load. "He don't do so well in all his classes like he does in yours." She shrugged. "He don't do so well in summer school either."

Lani grimaced sympathetically.

"I'm sorry about that Mrs. Begay. I wish I could help, but there's not much I can do about summer school."

Ozzie tugged at Lani's shirt.

"They don't let me cut class like you do."

"Ummm ... Let's call it independent study, Ozzie. Not cutting class."

"Yeah. They just make me sit there. It's boring. I wish I could cut like I did in your class—"

"Independent study, Ozzie."

"Yeah, but Mom says she'll whup me if I do."

"I don't care what you call it," Mrs. Begay said. "You let him go in the forest and he reads books about the outdoors."

"*Call of the Wild!*" Ozzie shouted.

"Yeah. And you finished it. But the other teachers, they make him sit at a desk and he doesn't read anything. I know what works. But I don't want him held back."

Lani smiled.

"I don't blame you. He won't get through school doing his own thing, I'm sorry to say. The schools want everybody learning the same way, even if it doesn't work for all the kids. I try to give my own students a little more space."

"Yeah. I wish there was more like you."

"Thanks."

Not wanting to spend the entire day chatting with a former student's mother, Lani dropped her eyes to her shopping list. She hoped she wasn't being too rude, but she had chores to do.

"Hey."

Lani's eyes rose—and froze. The box of feminine pads she'd tossed in her cart was being roughly examined from between Mrs. Begay's large, calloused hands.

"You use these? Don't they hurt?"

Lani bent her lips into a weak smile.

Chapter 5

W hen Lani arrived at Scott's house, Champ, as usual, surged ahead, straining at the leash.

"Take it easy, boy. You'll see Scott in a minute."

She hauled back on Champ's leash, pitting her 120 pound against Champ's 65 pounds of slobbering enthusiasm, to allow herself enough reach to wriggle her hands into her purse for her keys to Scott's house. With the maneuver accomplished, she allowed the black-and-white mutt to lead the way to Scott's back door. Champ promptly nosed the door open, snatched the leash from Lani's hand, and disappeared into the house.

Lani glanced at the splintered rear door frame, then at the keys in her hand.

"Scott!"

She passed through the kitchen, glancing at the polished wooden cabinets on the wall. The kitchen had been a sore spot when she and Scott began dating—actually, it was how they began dating.

Dragged from bed early one morning by the sound of a power saw screaming its way through lumber, she'd quickly dressed in the previous day's clothes, left scattered on her bedroom floor. The narrow hallway of her cluttered cottage was lined with shelves crowded mostly with children's books. Gaps showed where books had been loaned to students.

Trotting behind her, Champ whimpered with concern. Recently acquired from a shelter where he'd landed after being found wandering the street dirty and emaciated, the dog had quickly attached himself to Lani. He'd also demonstrated his appreciation for his new home and good treatment by taking a proprietary interest in the woman's well-being. One of Lani's more-aggressive dates learned the extent of Champ's devotion when he talked his way through the door and tried to force the evening past her comfort zone. Lani sincerely hoped Champ's teeth left permanent scars.

Now she rarely went anyplace without him. She grabbed the dog's leash from a peg by the front door.

Five-feet, two-inches of blonde fury, she'd stalked across the driveway to the newly purchased neighboring house with Champ by her side. She'd marched to the back door, from behind which the cacophony seemed to originate. She'd put her full body weight into pounding on the door. A tall, muscular, balding man wearing dirty cut-off shorts and protective goggles pushed to the top of his head, with raccoon eyes of clean skin surrounded by an even layer of sawdust, answered her knock.

"What can I do for you?"

"I live next door. Right next door. Do you have any idea what time it is?"

The man shifted his gaze to a wall clock mounted above the arch leading to the living room. It's ... *whoops*! It's just 6. Sorry if I woke you up. I couldn't sleep and I thought it was later."

Lani glanced around the construction zone that had replaced the house's kitchen. Out of the corner of her eye, she caught Champ easing forward and sniffing curiously at the stranger. The dog grinned. She tugged back on the leash.

"You're renovating?"

"Yep."

"I don't see a permit posted."

"I don't have one."

"You may not know, but the city requires—"

The man shook his head and interrupted.

"I know, but I don't care. The city doesn't own this house. I do. The mayor doesn't have to ask my permission to make city hall even uglier than it already is, and I'm not gonna ask his permission to install some cabinets and an electric oven that won't burn my dinner."

Lani stood at the doorstep with her mouth open. Then she smiled.

"You don't like being told what to do, do you?"

The half-dressed man smiled back.

"Nope. But I also don't like bugging people. I'm really sorry about that."

He reached out of Lani's sight and grabbed a t-shirt as ratty as his shorts. As he slipped the shirt over his head, Champ pushed forward and nuzzled the man's bare knee.

Lani quickly jerked back on the leash, harder than before.

"I guess we can call it a rough meeting. I'm Lani. I live in the house over there. And I usually get up right about now to go to my job as a teacher."

The man ruffled the fur on Champ's head with one hand and reached out the other.

"Pleased to meet you Lani. I'm Scott. I sleep at strange times when I'm not telecommuting to my office back east."

"You telecommute? What do you do?"

"I write and edit an online business magazine."

"You're a writer? Cool. Do you read a lot too?"

"Oh yeah. You should have heard the movers bitch about carrying my crates of books."

Lani smiled again. Actually, she stifled a laugh at his raccoon eyes. She coughed to cover a giggle.

"So … You moved here from back East?"

"Boston, most recently. I wanted a raise and easier access to the outdoors." Scott brushed at his forehead, leaving a flesh-colored streak in the sawdust. "I realized I could give myself both if I moved away from East Coast taxes and closer to the trails, and Flagstaff is surrounded by beautiful country. My boss thought that was a swell idea, since he could save a bundle on benefits by paying me as a contractor. Everybody walked away happy."

"Except for the tax collectors?"

"True." Scott smiled. "Making them cry is just gravy."

Lani snickered. Then she caught another glimpse of the wall clock.

"Oh. I have to get my day started. Maybe you could show me your book collection sometime."

"I'll be happy to. Hey—do you want breakfast? I make mean omelettes over a campstove."

He was right. The omelettes were good.

Scott was jigging with Champ when she turned the corner. Bare-chested, in sunglasses and a cowboy hat, he hopped up and down, feet flying, to whatever music flowed through the wire that disappeared under his hat. The dog leaped around him, making his own music of excited yelps. A stack of papers lay in disarray at the base of the fax machine.

"You look like a demented porn actor."

Scott doffed the hat and headphones. Something heavy on pipes and fiddles escaped into the room before he tapped his finger to pause the music.

"What's that, baby?"

"I said … never mind. Did you know that somebody forced your back door?"

Scott stopped jigging and bent to pet Champ. The dog responded to the attention by flopping on his back, exposing his belly for a rub.

"Yep. Rollo dropped by for a visit. He'll fix the lock later."

Lani made a face, and then bent to land a kiss on Scott's lips that left them just shy of bruised. She unhooked the leash still trailing from Champ's collar.

"Is he still living on Forest Service land?"

"It's not the Forest Service's land, much as they'd like us to think otherwise. But no, for now he seems to be living on my sofa."

"What?" Lani shot to her feet. She felt her face flushing with blood. "No fucking way!"

Scott stood quickly, stepping back as if to give himself a safe clearance from Lani's stabbing finger. He held his hands high and apart in a defensive posture.

Champ languished on the floor, belly to the sky, wondering at the loss of all of the attention he'd enjoyed just a moment before.

"I didn't say he's moving in; he just needs a place to crash until he … uh … finds himself another den or something."

Lani closed her eyes and breathed deeply, then looked back at Scott. There were times when she really didn't understand the guy. Here was a smart man with a house and a life hanging around with a crazy old hobo. Why?

"What happened to the rat hole he was living in?"

Scott smirked.

"It got de-ratted. The Forest Service burned him out and stole his truck."

Lani reached with her left hand to scratch gently between Champ's ears. Unwilling to lie on the floor waiting for people to come to him, he had stood and now leaned his full weight against his owner's legs, content in the knowledge that now he couldn't be ignored.

"What? What do you mean the Forest Service 'burned him out'?"

Scott shrugged. He reached to shut off his computer, closing down software and then tapping the "Start" icon to power the system down.

"I just know what he told me. The rangers found his latest shack. He ran away before they could catch him. As he was driving away in one of their trucks he saw smoke rising from where the shack was."

Lani cocked her head.

"Rollo stole a Forest Service truck?"

Scott shrugged again, then wandered from the office toward the kitchen. Lani heard him rummaging in the refrigerator. Freeing herself from the dog's weight—Champ flopped to the floor as if he'd been rendered boneless—she wandered into the kitchen herself just in time to see Scott guzzling from an orange juice carton.

"Hey," Scott called to her. "It was a fair trade. The rangers got to keep that old junker he was driving around."

"Yeah, right. Y'know, if he wasn't your friend, I'd have called the cops on him a long time ago."

Scott casually stuffed the carton back in the refrigerator.

"Baby, if he wasn't my friend, you wouldn't know anything about his intriguing activities."

Rather than concede the point, Lani changed subjects.

"Do you have much more work to do today?"

Scott winced, doffed his hat and ran the fingers of his right hand through the tightly cropped fuzz that represented the last stand of his hairline.

"Oh, that's the other thing I have to tell you. I finally got fired. Right in the middle of the meeting—I had a meeting today, by the way—Todd and that bimbo shadow of his start pointing out that I really have nothing left to do since they downsized my department into an expensive photocopying operation."

Lani buried her face in her hands.

"Anyway, I turned it around on Todd and asked what his responsibilities are."

"Did you get him fired too?"

Scott shook his head.

"Nope! It turns out the jerk has a lot of responsibility. He sounds pretty productive too. Who knew?"

Chapter 6

Ranger Jason Hewitt of the National Forest Service (Richard Wilson District) squirmed on the plastic seat of the cheap tubular-steel chair. His face, above the collar of his green polyester button-down shirt, was smudged and a strong odor of wood smoke hung about him.

"Strictly speaking," he began, a little hesitantly, "we don't *know* what happened to my vehicle."

"No," a slightly scratchy, nasal voice interrupted. "We don't *know* what happened to your vehicle." Jason's own emphasis on "know" was repeated, but drawn out with singsong quality that made the ranger wince.

Jason wished he were somewhere, anywhere else than across a desk from his boss and co-conspirator, Chief Ranger Martin Van Kamp.

Van Kamp sat tall behind his battered sheet metal desk—tall, that is, on an office chair cranked all the way to the top of its elevatory capacity, and then a bit taller on a Phoenix telephone book placed on the cushion. His full five-foot, four-inch, 125-pound frame bounced in agitation atop its makeshift throne.

"But we can make an educated guess now, can't we?"

Jason nodded.

"Do you think an elk made off with your vehicle?" Van Kamp rasped.

Jason shook his head.

"Maybe a hawk? Perhaps a red-tailed hawk hot-wired your Chevy Blazer and hauled it off to a chop shop?"

Jason grimaced and raised both hands in front of him like a shield. "Actually, the keys were in the ignition."

Van Kamp pulled up short—shorter anyway.

"Keys were in the ignition," he repeated, seeming to exhale the phrase through his nostrils.

Jason nodded.

"So, pretty much anybody could have made off with your truck."

Van Kamp leaned forward in his chair, face red and nostrils flaring. An image of an enraged baboon passed through Jason's mind and he involuntarily hunched in his chair, bracing for attack.

"Except that the only fucking person out there, other than your team, was the squatter you were supposed to be grabbing."

"As far as we know," Jason protested, drawing his legs up on the chair as Van Kamp leaned forward across his desk.

"Jason, the squatter was out there because there's nobody else around. Your vehicle disappeared from a wash a couple of hundred yards from his shack. I think there's a really good chance he's now driving around northern Arizona in a Forest Service-issue Chevy Blazer."

Knees under his chin, arms folded across his shins, Jason couldn't even nod acknowledgment. He made do with a whimper.

The office fell silent for several minutes as Van Kamp came to terms with his rage and Jason grappled with his fear.

Happy thoughts, Jason told himself. Think happy thoughts. He visualized a world of pristine wilderness where forests and deserts were untouched by the hand of man—no people, anywhere.

Except for him!

There he was, deep in the forest, naked, with no man-made implements of any sort to sully nature's purity. He was somehow taller in his vision, more muscular than the image he saw in the mirror in the morning.

Wait! And there runs a deer. It's a beautiful white-tail doe. Such soft fur. Such limpid eyes. Come here you pretty–

"Um hmmm," Van Kamp cleared his throat. "Do you have anything to say?"

Jason's eye snapped open and he shuddered at the view in front of him.

"Uh yeah. There's no reason why we can't still pin the fire on the squatter. The fact that he stole a government vehicle should make it even more believable on top of the fact that he was trespassing on public land."

"We'll do that. It'd be a lot easier if we had him in custody, and if we were sure that he didn't see you light that fire. Chances are the cops will find him anyway. We'll have him nailed as an arsonist and a car thief. Even if he saw something, nobody will believe a word he says."

"You bet!" Jason nodded. His eyes took on a bright glint. "After the Carthage Option cleanses the land, people will want this guy to hang."

Van Kamp rolled his eyes.

"Uh ... yeah. All right, get out of here—and be more careful. We can't afford any witnesses."

"Will do."

"And stop throwing around that 'Carthage Option' crap. Jesus, but that's a bit obvious."

Jason nodded, but repeated the phrase to himself. Carthage Option. Carthage Option. He really liked the way it sounded—like he was a secret agent on a mission.

Van Kamp rose again in his seat, leaning toward his cowering underling.

"Now get that damned truck out of the front of my building."

Jason unfolded his legs, letting blood flow back into the extremities he'd clutched so tightly. Hobbling on tingling feet, he eagerly fled Van Kamp's office, then set to figuring out how to extract an old, junked pickup truck from a cinderblock wall. Stranded as his team had been in the forest after their Blazer was stolen, they'd fled the fire with the only vehicle at hand—Rollo's junker.

It wasn't until Jason and his team arrived at the Forest Service office that they discovered the old truck's handicap in the matter of brakes.

Chapter 7

That evening, Rollo wandered back to Scott's house by foot, following a weaving course through the streets leading to the small stone- and wood-sided cottage. He sipped slowly at a beer smuggled to the street from a downtown bar and enjoyed the pleasant glow of a day of vice in the city. In his left hand was a paper bag sporting a hardware store logo.

He gave a sharp rap to Scott's front door with the base of the beer bottle, and then let himself in through the unlocked entryway. Within seconds he found himself warding off Champ, who launched an enthusiastic greeting directly at his crotch and could be dissuaded only with a vigorous scratch behind the ears.

A flurry of motion caught Rollo's eye as he entered the living room. He made out a brief glimpse of something slim and blonde in mid-leap from Scott's lap.

"Nice tits, Lani," Rollo said. He chuckled as the woman promptly pulled and tugged at the top of her sports bra. He hadn't actually caught a glimpse of anything, but he never passed up a chance to needle his friend's girlfriend.

"Did you find another refrigerator box to live in?" Lani shot back.

Scott remained motionless, sprawled across the sofa, a broad grin spreading across his face. He wore running shorts and a t-shirt. He and Lani both looked like they'd been through a workout. For Scott's sake Rollo hoped it was the same kind of workout he himself had enjoyed not long ago, especially since the younger man didn't have to pay for his fun in hard cash.

"Hey, Rollo," Scott called out. "You're looking shaved, showered and happy. I take it you found what you were looking for."

"Yep," Rollo answered. "Flagstaff is still worth a damn after all."

Lani looked back and forth between the two.

"I'm not sure what you guys are talking about, but I'll bet it's disgusting."

"What we're talking about?" Rollo asked, raising his eyebrows. "I'm sorry, I should have been clearer. I went to a whorehouse and got my pipes cleaned. Then I went to a bar and got piss drunk. Which I am now. Well, I would be if I could still drink without feeling like crap. Actually, I barely have a buzz."

Scott doubled over in laughter.

"You really *are* disgusting." Lani folded her arms and leaned back on the sofa, distancing herself from both men.

Mostly recovered from his bout of hilarity, Scott jumped in.

"Is that my new back door latch?" He pointed to the bag in Rollo's hand.

"Yep. Get me a beer and put some music on the radio and I'll go make your house safe and secure. Well, as safe and secure as it was before I broke in. Heh."

Scott rose from the sofa and headed for the kitchen, followed by Rollo and his paper bag. Champ trailed them both, grinning and wide-eyed with hope that whatever the two men had planned would involve food.

"We're out of beer. You can have water or ... huh ... water.

That OK?"

Rollo sniffed in disgust.

"Yeah, water is OK."

Lani remained unmoving on the sofa, her arms still folded. After a long 30 seconds of snubbing an empty room, during which time Rollo and Scott chatted in the kitchen and Champ flopped on the tile floor in disappointment, she sighed, hopped off the sofa and turned on the stereo beneath the TV set in the knotty pine entertainment center.

In the kitchen, Rollo sat on the floor, staring in dismay at the doorframe. The frame was truly a mess, with the brass lock plate hanging free and a spray of splinters where he'd shoved the bolt through the wood. His head hurt too. He knew he shouldn't have had that last beer.

"Damn, I'm strong." He raised his right arm and flexed his bicep. He accompanied the gesture with a weak grin.

Scott, standing over him, grunted. Then he sipped at the glass in his hand.

"Y'know, you're making me nervous standing there. And isn't that my water?"

Scott handed the glass down, but didn't budge an inch.

With the edge of a putty knife, the seated mountain man pried open a can of wood putty and scooped out a generous blob.

"No," Scott said.

"What?"

"No. You're not gluing that mess back together with wood putty."

"Well, what the Hell do you want me to do?"

Scott stared around the kitchen, tapping his foot at the same time.

"Hell. Tomorrow we'll go get some lumber and reframe the door. You'll earn your keep fixing this the right way."

Rollo sighed.

"Fair enough."

With a patter of bare feet, Lani burst into the kitchen.

"Guys, there's something about a wildfire on the radio. It's out near Williams." She glanced at Rollo.

"I told you!" Rollo yelled, jumping up. He was happy to be free of his locksmithing duties. "Those bastards burned me out. Now it's out of control."

"They say they think it was started by a vagrant," Lani added, still looking at Rollo.

Rollo turned to face Lani, then wagged a finger and spoke softly. "Lani, I am a lot of things. But I'm not so dumb that I'm going to set fire to my own back yard."

The room was silent for a long moment, then Scott took Lani by the arm.

"I believe him," Scott said. "Vagrants may start fires, but Rollo isn't a vagrant; he's a feral weirdo. He knows what he's doing. Let's see what else we can find out."

Chapter 8

Leaping from treetop to treetop, the flames roared across the land. Sucked dry by years of drought, weakened from infestation by bark beetles, and crowded by well-intentioned but ill-considered fire-suppression tactics that prevented small fires from burning brush and thinning the press of trees, the ponderosa forest of northern Arizona had become, potentially, the world's largest barbecue pit.

The fire was reported only after it had burned for several days—unusually late, considering the close watch kept for smoke and flames that could herald a catastrophic wildfire. When firefighters finally arrived, they quickly established lines intended to keep the fire away from populated areas and set back-burns meant to consume fuel that would otherwise become part of the wildfire.

Line after line was breached, with fire inexorably jumping ahead and establishing new beachheads. In an area of thin habitation, the flames moved, almost as if with a purpose, through open forest, then outlying settlements, toward the town of Williams and its roughly 3,000 residents.

Far from the office of the red-faced, excitable chief ranger, Jason felt at-home. There was nobody here to screech and point fingers. He was in his beloved forest, which he expected would heal from the flames that were already driving out the human invaders.

Smudged from head-to-toe, Jason surveyed his half-dozen equally sooty colleagues. There were Ray and Tim, in matching crewcuts and aviator sunglasses. Both men nursed aspirations to work for the FBI, but had somehow ended up in the Park Service instead. They might not actually be G-Men, but they could act the role, which was sometimes a little disconcerting—especially when they were leading children's tours at the Grand Canyon. Even so, they were really good at taking orders and viewed any civilian off pavement as a potential security threat.

Terry was a fellow Forest Service ranger who shared Jason's proprietary view of wide-open spaces.

And then came Bob, Rena and Samantha, volunteers from the Center for Floral Supremacy who'd bicycled all the way up from Tucson under orders from Rupert Greenfield, their group's bearded, cult-like leader. The trio had recovered from severe dehydration, suffered during their ride through the desert, on the floor of Jason's conscripted living room while Greenfield, Van Kamp and other people Jason didn't know cooked up the plan that Jason insisted on calling the Carthage Option. Bob, Rena and Samantha were so pure in their dedication to the shared vision of a human-free wilderness, and so neglectful of mere civilized concerns, such as hygiene, that Jason found them a little intimidating.

All of them wore Forest Service uniforms like his, to discourage questions about their presence near a wildfire.

Would there be room for them all in the new wilderness? Jason suddenly wondered. They were good, earnest people, but he hoped they wouldn't crowd him in the world they were making. Maybe he'd have to do something about that; he'd pick and choose among his allies.

Like Samantha. He could imagine sharing the forest with Samantha. She was almost doe-eyed … He lost himself in thought, gazing once again down at the hypnotizing flames.

The members of the small group all stared, slightly wild-eyed, from the temporary safety of a ridge to their ravenous handiwork below.

It's not easy being radical green, Jason thought to himself.

Chapter 9

Two days after Jason looked out over his handiwork, Martin Van Kamp sat sweating and uncomfortable in a stuffy motel room. The diminutive Forest Service administrator sipped at a paper cup of tepid tapwater while trying to find a non-lumpy spot on the bed. His feet barely touched the floor, giving him little leverage to shift his position. So, in his search for a soft perch, he had to hop on his buttocks from position to position, probing for a few square inches that didn't feel like a sack of old laundry. The room in the low-rent motel jammed in along Flagstaff's Route 66 strip of cut-rate conveniences for travelers on a budget certainly *smelled* like a sack of old laundry, or at least like a high school locker room.

Looking equally uncomfortable, Van Kamp's counterparts from the Bureau of Land Management and the National Park Service leaned back in the small room's two rickety chairs. In rumpled uniforms pasted to their bodies by the ongoing heat wave, and unrefreshed by even the slightest breeze—the room's one window was sealed tight, with the blinds closed—they glanced occasionally at the TV whispering softly on its veneer tabletop, but clearly preferred keeping an eye on Van Kamp's acrobatic antics.

Surrendering to the inevitable, Van Kamp ended his search for a soft spot on the mattress, preferring a measure of dignity to a quixotic quest for comfort in a room that seemed to stand as a shrine to the motel management's relaxed attitude toward housekeeping.

His colleagues were clearly disappointed, and the three turned their gazes to the television.

The screen was occupied by a lined, bearded face haloed by a spray of graying hair and partially obscured by the word "LIVE" in excessively large, fire-engine red letters. He looked like a biblical prophet who'd been tracked, sedated, and stuffed into an off-the-rack Sears sport coat.

The screen briefly flashed to a pretty, redheaded interviewer who appeared to be crowding the upper end of her teen years, then switched back to the bearded face.

"Absolutely!" the face said in a voice that, even at the volume's lowest setting, caused the three men in the room to glance warily toward the door. "The tragedy in Williams proves that there are places where human habitation is doomed." He dragged out the "oo" in "doomed" like an actor in a late-night horror movie. "The high desert is no place for crowds of people in their houses and SUVs. The forest needs to burn to refresh itself, and it will burn no matter who is there and no matter what is in its path."

"So, do you expect more wildfires like this—?"

"Nobody can predict the future," the face answered, leaning forward and shaking his head with the certainty of his prophetical demeanor. "But the human population of Arizona's rural areas has hit critical mass and that means more fire started by nature and by people who have no business in the wilderness, and more homes to be burned by that fire. Nature will take its own course, and that portends an end to mammalian dominance in northern Arizona."

"Oh shit," the BLM official muttered in the fetid motel room.

The interviewer blinked blankly with her mouth half open. The moment drew out, uncomfortably long.

"Thank you so much for your time, Dr. Greenfield. Now,

back to—"

A few seconds later, the motel room door opened inwards, revealing the bearded man and a brief glimpse of the TV interviewer chatting with a cameraman in the motel parking lot. The three men in the room all leaned forward for a glance at the interviewer's legs below her skirt, Van Kamp almost toppling from the bed in the process.

"Holy shit," the bearded man said, stripping off the sports jacket and tossing it toward the head of the bed. "If the TV crews around here get any younger, they'll need diapers and a changing table in the van."

"They're college kids," Van Kamp explained. "The station saves money—"

"Never mind that," the BLM official said. "What's this 'mammalian dominance' crap? I thought you were going to can the weirdness and stay on-message."

"Stuff it, you little bureaucrat. If it wasn't for me, you'd never have had the balls—"

While the prophet and the BLM official argued, Van Kamp and his Park Service counterpart peeped through the blinds to see the television crew loading their equipment into a van prominently marked with the local TV station's logo. Free from fear of discovery, they wrestled the room's two windows open and gasped for fresh air.

Revived, Van Kamp turned to face the room. "Enough. All Greenfield was supposed to do was set the tone. How he does that is his business." He turned back to the window for a quick breath, then faced the room once again. "With Williams burned out, people are already on edge. Greenfield's little performance will scare the shit out of them."

"So the next step—" the BLM official began.

"The next step is the next fire. My office has already put out an alert about a small blaze west of Flagstaff. That gave us a reason to seal the roads out there. I've assigned a trusted crew to make sure there *is* a fire. In no time at all, the highway will be clogged with panicked families looking for a soft, safe hidey-hole far from the dangerous forest."

His eyes burning into his colleagues, Greenfield nodded his head and spoke.

"And all of this beautiful country around us will return to the wilderness it was meant to be, untroubled by wrongful incursions." After a pause, he added, "Except for the damned mammals."

"And the people assigned to protect that vulnerable wilderness are likely to get a lot more money and power than they've had in the past," Van Kamp added.

Greenfield, Van Kamp, the BLM official and the Park Service man all glanced at each other, then smiled. Visions, respectively, of a human-free utopia and of supplementary budgets danced in their heads.

Finally, the Park Service man spoke.

"Can we please turn on the air conditioner?" His voice betrayed a slight whine.

Van Kamp and the BLM official nodded in relief, each happy to not be the one who broke first.

Greenfield looked at them all in disgust.

"Wimps."

Chapter 10

The restaurant at the Weatherford Hotel was unusually crowded for a weekday lunchtime. Three families shuffled around the small, history-laden lobby, glancing at photographs of Flagstaff in its timber-driven heyday and waiting for tables.

Scott caught the manager's eye.

"What's going on, Ron? Some kind of university event?"

Short and slim, with dark hair graying at the temples, Ron shook his head.

"Lani, Scott, good to see you guys." Then he leaned in close and spoke in a barely audible whisper.

"They're mostly Williams people. The Red Cross has them camped out in the high school gyms, and they're wandering through town looking for something to do."

Ron backed up and grabbed two menus.

"Hang on. I'll get you guys a table." He disappeared into the main dining room.

"Is he actually setting up another table for us," Lani asked.

"I think so. Hey, he has a major crush on you. It comes in handy."

"You don't know that," Lani answered. But she blushed.

"I have a pretty good idea. It's OK. I take it as a compliment to you—and to my taste in picking you."

"Oh, so *you* picked *me*."

"Or maybe it was the other way around. Which would only go to show that you have excellent taste yourself."

"Speaking of taste ... Today's meal is on me. Let's call it a freedom-from-employment lunch."

"Well ... sure. How can I turn down a celebration of imminent destitution?"

Ron reappeared with the menus in his hand.

"Come on guys."

One of the men in the lobby, decked out in boots, a cowboy hat and brown, leathery skin, looked like he was going to protest. His wife, in blue jeans and with an outdoorsy complexion to match, put her hand on his arm. The man's gaze dropped to the toes of his boots and his entire body seemed to sag. He looked like a deflated balloon. Scott nudged Lani ahead of him and brushed by as quickly as he could.

"I can't even imagine," he said. "That fire took everything."

"I can't either."

Ron escorted them through the dining room to the outdoor seating area along Leroux Street. A tiny two-top crowded a corner, partially projecting under the light chain that separated the area from the public sidewalk.

"Thanks, Ron."

The manager's eyes were spot-welded to Lani as he helped her wriggle into a chair between a post supporting the upstairs balcony and another diner. A goofy grin clung to his face as the woman writhed inside her tight t-shirt in an effort to take her seat.

"I said thanks, Ron."

"Oh, no problem. I'll have Pam out to take your order."

Scott chuckled as the manager disappeared into the dining room.

Lani blushed again.

"OK, you're right. Just shut up about it."

Still chuckling, Scott turned his attention to the street. After his conversation with Ron, he viewed the street traffic with a different eye. The usual tourists and college kids still prowled the few scant blocks of Flagstaff's downtown area. Middle-aged couples popped in and out of trinket shops; teens and twenty-somethings wheeled bicycles along the sidewalk under the bored gaze of two city police officers. But another element was added to the mix.

Concentrated in Heritage Square, whole families clustered and wandered about. They mostly had the leathery, sun-soaked look of people who spent lots of time outdoors as a matter of course. Cowboy boots and hats abounded, as did belt-buckles large enough to eat off of and facial hair that proudly spurned any restraint.

These were Williams folks all right.

Scott didn't know a lot about Williams, but he knew it was an old railroad town that, in recent years, relied on Grand Canyon-bound tourism to keep itself from drying up and blowing away. He doubted the scorched town's refugees had much in the way of resources to fall back on with their homes and possessions burned.

He started as Lani's hand closed over his.

"What do you want to eat, hon?"

"Oh. Navajo taco, please. And a wheat beer." The beer was brewed just down the street in one of the town's three brewpubs.

Lani ordered a chicken sandwich and an iced tea for herself.

Ron reappeared with the drinks in his hand. He set them down on the glass tabletop to which streams of condensation instantly flowed to form tiny moats.

"Hey, I meant to tell you earlier."

"Yeah?"

"Your hobo friend—"

"Rollo?"

That's him. Rollo. Anyway, he was in earlier, and things got a little ugly in the bar."

"Rollo was born ugly."

Ron emitted a short giggle, his eyes on Lani the entire time. She shot him a brief smile, then sipped at her tea. She flashed a quick wink at Scott.

"Ron, I'm over here. So there was a problem in the bar."

"Uh huh. Some of the Williams people recognized him—I guess he spends some time in town there. Anyway, the word is out that he might have started the fire, and a guy who'd had a few decided he wanted a piece of Rollo."

"Was anybody hurt?"

"The drunk, but not badly. Rollo's pretty tough. We hustled them both out of the bar."

Scott sighed.

"Thanks. I'll keep an eye on him."

"It's probably not a great time for him to be wandering around Flag."

"I'll let him know."

For moments after the manager walked away, the table remained silent. Scott sipped at his beer, and Lani watched.

"You really watch out for him, don't you?"

"Rollo?"

"Yes."

"Somebody has to. He's half feral; he can just about barely function in modern society. If it was 1850, he'd be fine wandering back and forth between town and the forest. But people today like things squeaky clean and tightly regulated. Rollo doesn't have a regular job or address by choice—he's not a charity case. That makes people nervous."

"Me too, I guess."

"Well ... you and he have never gotten along. I think at some level you resent him doing what he damned well pleases, and at some level you're afraid that I'm going to disappear into the forest with him to hunt elk and live like Daniel Boone. I'm not, you know. I like electricity too much, and I love you."

Lani extended her hand across the table; Scott took it in his own.

"Thank you," she said. "That might be it. You are similar in some ways. You did slash that cop's tire together."

"Well, that was my idea. That's how he and I met."

"I know. Let's not share that story with too many people."

Scott hadn't picked a policeman randomly, but he hadn't really planned the caper either. He'd been driving east along Route 66, on his way to pick up some things for Lani, his then-new girlfriend, when he was pulled over for speeding. Traffic was light after work hours, and his foot had probably been a little heavy on the gas pedal with nothing but open road ahead, so he'd bit his tongue when the officer walked up to his car window.

But he hadn't been able to keep a slight grimace from tightening his lips, and that grimace set off a five-minute lecture about proper civilian decorum toward officers of the law.

Still smarting from that tongue-lashing an hour later, Scott spotted the same cop getting out of his patrol car on a residential street. Without really thinking, he pulled his pocketknife from his jeans—a semi-custom monster with a curved 5 1/2-inch blade and a push-button locking mechanism—crossed the street after a careful look in all directions, and stuck the blade deep into the rubber of the left front tire.

"Need a hand?"

Scott looked up to meet the cheerful eyes of a long-haired, middle-aged man toting an enormous backpack. Unless something had gone terribly wrong with the police department's uniform budget, this wasn't a cop.

"Sure. Pick a tire."

Afterward, they'd gone for a drink.

But that was then. Now, the arrival of the lunch order briefly interrupted the couple's conversation. Digging in to his meal, Scott paused with a full fork half way to his mouth.

"You don't have to like Rollo, but don't hate him because you think I'm going to join his barbarian tribe. You're stuck with me."

Lani stood to lean across the table and kissed Scott on the lips, jarring his hand in the process. They both laughed as his first sample of lunch landed in his lap.

"I don't consider it 'stuck,'" she said. "I'm happy we're together. You have good qualities—a few, anyway."

Chapter 11

Rollo was at Scott's house when he heard a nearly word-for-word broadcast of Van Kamp's press release about a new wildfire during a newsbreak on the local classic rock radio station. He was sitting grumpily on Scott's sofa, nursing a beer and a grudge—partially because his music tastes were now archaic enough to be considered "classic." He was afraid to venture back into town after the barroom near-brawl and the subsequent warning he'd received from his host.

Flagstaff was clogged with refugees from Williams. The refugees were at loose ends, wandering the streets, passing time in the bars and looking for somebody to blame for the charcoal pit that now occupied the one-time site of "the gateway to the Grand Canyon."

The Forest Service claimed that a vagrant set the fire that destroyed Williams. Much to his disgust, Rollo, who thought of himself as a throwback to the bold days of Bill Williams and other early mountain men, found himself fitting the official description of the suspect.

So on Scott's sofa Rollo slumped, his plaid shirt unbuttoned halfway to his navel, revealing a puff of graying hair and a slight paunch. He sank deeper into depression while the J. Geils Band's

Centerfold thumped from the stereo speakers.

Christ, I'm horny, he thought.

Two minutes later, he barged into Scott's office.

"There's beer in the fridge," Scott said upon the rushed arrival of his friend. He didn't even look up. Scott was seated at his desk with his nose buried in his checkbook and a legal pad covered with numbers and scratch marks under his right hand. A stack of paperback books, hemmed in by the last fax sent to Scott's former employers and a lightweight rain jacket reduced to the size of a small submarine sandwich within a tightly stuffed small nylon bag, teetered on the desk's edge. Sitting atop a collection of Terry Southern's dope- and madness-fueled essays, Claire Wolfe's *101 Things To Do 'til The Revolution* capped the stack, pinned in place by the .45-caliber paperweight.

"Don't clean me out," Scott continued. "There's not much more on the way."

Agitated, Rollo barked. "No, that's not it."

"Well, what then?"

"According to the radio news, there's a new fire on the west side of town."

Scott looked up from his financial labors.

"That sucks," he said.

"You don't get it," answered Rollo, growing even more agitated. "If those khaki—"

"Khaki-shirted bastards?" Scott interrupted.

Rollo ignored him.

"If they can set a fire to burn out Williams, why wouldn't they do the same thing to Flagstaff?"

Scott leaned back in his swiveling office chair, testing its hinges and posing a challenge to gravity. He ran the fingers of his right hand through the tightly cropped stubble atop his head.

"Because, maybe they didn't do it to Williams." he said. "At least, not deliberately. I mean, accidentally burning a town to the ground during an office cook-out is like the Forest Service. A carefully executed nefarious scheme really isn't."

Stretched tight over clenched teeth, Rollo's thin lips turned white. He crossed his arms over his chest and huffed and snorted through his nose.

Scott sighed.

"All right, what do you want to do?"

Within half an hour, Rollo, Scott and an impressive assortment of backpacking gear were loaded into the stolen Chevy Blazer.

"Where did you get that license plate," Scott asked.

"Off a truck in the City Hall parking lot. I figure anybody spending much time in that building is up to no good."

"It's a nice touch. It complements the new primer finish you slapped over the government-issue puke color."

Thrust into a holster and firmly fastened with a Velcro strap to a backpack hipbelt, Scott's large-caliber paperweight added its reassuring mass to the equipment list.

Upon Scott's insistence, they invited Lani to join the expedition.

"You're crazy," she told them. "Why would I want to go barging with you into an area the Forest Service sealed off. Isn't that illegal?"

"A misdemeanor, at least," Scott answered. "But school is out, you're bored, and I'll be there. Don't you want to keep me out of trouble."

"Maybe."

"Bring your backpacking gear."

"What? Why?"

"Just in case."

Before Lani formally consented, Champ had accepted his

unspoken invitation. He sat at Scott's feet, tail wagging and eyes wide, doggie backpack firmly clenched between his teeth. He knew when adventure was afoot.

Chapter 12

Had he known of Scott's assessment of his employer's scheming abilities, Jason might have grudgingly agreed. Assigned to start a fire in the forest near Flagstaff that would threaten to turn the city into a 63-square-mile weenie roast, he'd gathered his eager gang of rangers and volunteers, loaded two Forest Service trucks with personnel and gear, and headed out of town.

"Where are the drip torches?" Terry asked from behind one of the parked trucks along dusty, unpaved Forest Road 538. The warm vanilla smell of ponderosa pine trees brushed across the group, carried on a breeze that blew toward the San Francisco peaks. The mountains—really the shattered remnants of a huge, long-ago erupted volcano—towered above the treetops. The small city of Flagstaff, invisible from this perspective, nestled in assumed security at the base of promontories supposedly retired from the excesses of their explosive youth.

Aside from the sweet odor of the trees, the air rustled crystal-clear through branches and dry grass, untainted by dust or, more importantly, smoke.

Fire-resistant nomex coat draped over one arm, shaggy brown hair poking out from under his red hardhat, Terry hoped to correct that lack of taint.

But that would be hard to do without the proper equipment.

"Drip torches?" Jason asked, stalling for time. Then he gave it up. "Shit, we forgot the drip torches."

Standing side-by-side like crew-cut bookends, compact Sig pistols dangling from their hips, Ray and Tim adopted simultaneous looks of disgust. Jason ignored them. He was less successful at brushing off Samantha's look of blank-faced confusion.

"All right, everybody back in the trucks."

"Back in the trucks," Tim repeated in disbelief. "Why?"

"We're going back to town for our equipment."

And back they drove along FR538 toward FR231, which took a straight run past the arboretum, gained a layer of pavement and a name—Woody Mountain Road—and, after many miles eventually ran headlong into Route 66 on the west side of Flagstaff. But Jason grew more nervous the more ground disappeared beneath his truck's wheels. Fire had been announced to the good people of Flagstaff, but fire was nowhere to be seen. The sky was entirely too clear to herald any sort of impending disaster.

Even before FR538 met FR231, Jason stood on his brakes and brought his truck to a sliding halt amidst a cloud of dust that flowed in through open windows and had his passengers coughing and gasping for breath. He jumped from the truck and ran back to the trailing vehicle.

"*What?*" screamed Tim, his face flushed and his eyes hidden behind sunglasses. A little high-strung at the best of times, the frustrated policer of campsites and sightseeing tours was clearly running out of patience.

"Um ... we're short on time, so I figure we should head back to the site and improvise."

"Improvise, fucking *improvise*," Tim fumed. Trapped in the vehicle with the fulminating ranger, Bob, Rena and Terry seemed to shrink in their seats.

The mini-convoy made an abrupt U-turn, and headed back along the forest road, leaving a plume of dust rising into the air.

Chapter 13

As dirt roads go, Woody Mountain Road is pretty well maintained—at least for the first few miles. The road is wide and relatively smooth. Curves are fairly gentle and the washboard and rock found further down the road is rare. This makes the road past the arboretum, then through ranch land and into national forest a tempting one to drive at high speed.

"Slow down," Lani said.

"Why?" Rollo asked. He was fiddling with the radio while, perfunctorily, keeping an eye on the road. To his disgust, he discovered that the radio didn't even deliver static, let alone music. He gave up on the tuning knob in time to give the steering wheel a vigorous spin and whiz by a pine tree with no less (and little more) than two fingernail-breadths to spare.

"Fucking radio," Rollo said. "You pick up a new car, you expect everything to work."

Sitting rigidly in the shotgun seat, right hand pressed stiffly against the dash, Scott grunted. "You did get the car at a substantial discount," he added.

"Because," Lani broke in, demanding attention for her concern, "you almost killed us, and we don't know where we're going or what we're looking for."

Rollo sighed.

"Well, there is that."

The Blazer slowed and Scott and Lani both visibly relaxed.

"Funny how we haven't seen any rangers on this road at all," Scott said. "There was nobody at the barrier, and we haven't seen any firefighting crews since."

"So you actually thought we *would* run into rangers?" Lani asked. "You brought me back here expecting us to get arrested?"

"I knew rangers were a possibility," Scott said. He cocked a thumb toward the cargo area of the truck. "The backpacks are our alibi. We were out for a couple of days and had no idea the area was closed off."

"Wait, so we're *not* going backpacking?"

Scott shrugged—a gesture mostly wasted in the tight confines of the truck.

"We're off on an adventure. We may go backpacking. We may get chased around by forest rangers. At least we're not sitting at my desk contemplating my new unemployment. And, if Rollo's firebugs are out here somewhere, we'll catch 'em in action."

Lani sighed. She stroked the fur around Champ's throat, distracting the dog not a bit from his slobbering, open-mouthed delight at being in motion. Left ear held erect, right ear folded down in an arrangement like a cocky doggie beret, Champ clearly didn't care where they were going—it was the trip that mattered.

"Speaking of which," Lani said, holding on to the seat tightly over a prolonged stretch of washboard road. "Assuming that the firebugs *are* out here, how do we make sure we see them before they see us?"

"Assuming." Rollo grumbled. "*Assuming*. They're out here all right." He turned his attention from the road to Scott and Lani; the woman silently pointed at the road with her right hand and rotated Rollo's head to face forward with her left.

"I'll tell you what," Rollo continued. "If we don't find those bastards torching the forest, I'll fix that backdoor of yours for free."

Scott slowly turned is head toward his friend. "You'll fix that backdoor—that you broke—for free, all right. That is, unless you want to find someplace else to stay."

Rollo chuckled, happy at getting a rise from Scott.

"I repeat," Lani said. "How do we find the firebugs? If they exist."

"Well, we'll have to look for— Huh," Scott answered. "What's that?"

In the distance, rising above the trees, was a plume of dust of the sort tossed up by cars on dry, unpaved Arizona roads.

Chapter 14

Anxious over the delay in his official mission of arboreal arson, Jason once again stood on his brakes and brought his truck to a skidding halt. Fine Arizona soil, bone dry in the sun-drenched intermission between monsoon rains, rose up in a cloud and settled gently on Jason and his passengers.

Somebody coughed.

Jason heard a car door slam just a moment before Tim appeared at his window. Tim's face was dust-encrusted, with the powdery dirt bizarrely blurring the line between skin and sunglasses.

"Jason, what the hell are you doing? We're nowhere near the site we picked."

Jason gaped, momentarily thrown by Tim's appearance.

"Ummm."

"What?"

"Ummm. I figured this was good enough. Why waste more time by heading down the road?"

Tim sighed, then turned to face back toward his own vehicle.

"All right! This is it! Everybody out!"

Jason hopped from the truck and stretched his legs.

Instructed to improvise, the crew set to ransacking the trucks and their own gear for anything that could be used to start a fire. Lighters and stove fuel containers were set in a small pile by the side of the road.

"Hey," Samantha called from the truck's tailgate. She held a short section of rubber hose in her hand. "I bet we could use this to siphon gas from the tanks."

"Great idea! Are you up to giving it a try?"

Samantha nodded. "I have powerful lungs from all the bike-riding I do. I can suck as long and hard as you want."

Jason smiled. He was in love.

Chapter 15

Scott had hoped to spot any backcountry road traffic by the dust clouds it inevitably raised, but the brown pall hovering over FR 538 not far from the intersection with Woody Mountain Road looked like the leavings of a dune buggy rally. It hung heavy in the sky and dimmed the sun.

"Jesus Christ," he said. "It looks like a convoy went through here."

Rollo eyed the sky doubtfully.

"Not real sneaky, are they?"

"Maybe they have nothing to be sneaky about," Lani offered.

Rollo snorted.

"Rollo, why don't you pull off here," Scott said. We'll stick the truck back in the trees. If there's some kind of a Forest Service jamboree going on back here, we probably don't want to barge in."

Once under cover, the three retrieved their gear from the back of the truck, hauling out three backpacks of varying size and weight. Scott and Lani both shrugged into small, relatively new packs with plastic drinking tubes snapped smartly to shoulder straps. Scott's pack also put his gun within easy reach once the hipbelt was buckled in place.

Rollo attached himself to a large, ancient external-frame pack held together with wire and duct tape. A canteen dangled from his shoulder and extra water bottles peeked from pockets on the pack bags.

Lani snapped a leash to Champ's collar to keep him from bounding off through the trees and alerting whoever drove along on the road ahead. Unhappy at the restraint, Champ strained at the collar, leaning far forward and breathing roughly, while Lani leaned back, holding the dog in place.

"Damn it, Champ!"

Rollo shot a look at the battling pair.

"Maybe the dog ain't such a good—"

"Cool it, Champ," Scott hissed.

The dog relaxed.

Chapter 16

Retrieved from their semi-permanent stations under seats and in the back of the Forest Service trucks, a sizeable collection of empty soda cans and sports drink bottles stood in rank along the sides of the vehicles, ready for their infusions of gasoline.

"Don't you people *recycle*?" Rena shrieked at the sight of the ancient containers. Her square-cut brown mop of hair shook with agitation.

"Well ... sometimes," Jason answered defensively. "Those aren't all mine," he added.

"The generic soda is definitely yours," Terry said. Skinny to the point of deformity, the ranger was almost lost in his baggy uniform shirt, which flapped around him in the breeze. "Nobody else drinks that stuff."

Terry turned his attention back to the garden hose in his hand, which trailed from the gas tank of one of the trucks to Samantha, who calmly dispensed gasoline into a Gatorade bottle.

"Hey Jason," Terry called out. "How do you want us to use this stuff? I mean, are we just going to pour it in the grass and spark it up?"

Jason hesitated at the question. He really hadn't thought much beyond getting the gas out of the trucks. "Torches," he said.

"What?" Terry asked. The entire group stopped what they were doing to look at him quizzically.

"We'll make torches, soak them in gasoline and use the torches to light the grass." Jason smiled smugly in satisfaction.

On the other side of one of the trucks, with just their crewcuts and dirt-caked sunglasses visible, Tim and Ray shot back looks of overt disgust.

"What the fuck are we supposed to make torches out of," Tim asked.

Pinned by their gazes, Jason looked around wildly.

"Branches and ... uh ... " He thought hard, mentally dredging the inventory of supplies for anything that could be used to soak up fuel. "Our shirts!"

Chapter 17

Scott considered himself an experienced woodsman. So did Lani for that matter, minus the "man," of course. Rollo didn't know anything *other* than woods, so far as anybody could tell. But you wouldn't have known it once they were five minutes into the trees.

"Umm ... Honey? Where's the truck from here?" Lani asked.

There was a long moment of silence.

"Honey?"

Scott sighed.

"Behind us. Somewhere."

"Behind us?"

"–ish. Rollo ... ?"

"Don't fucking ask me. I'm just following that dust cloud."

Lani sputtered.

"Seriously? How do you—?"

"Ssshh. I hear voices up ahead," Scott whispered. He placed his hand on Champ's head to calm the dog. "Let me go ahead to take a look."

Rollo shook his head. Under strain from the movement, his threadbare canvas hat threatened to fly off in multiple directions.

"Hey, *I'm* the mountain man, city boy. I'll go ahead."

Scott glanced at his shaggy buddy, then poked him in the

paunch with his right-hand index finger.

"You're the *fat* mountain man. I don't know what you've been doing out in these forests, but you're eating entirely too well."

Rollo looked like he'd been stung. He patted his plaid shirt-encased belly with both hands

"Hey, there are goodies everywhere if you know where to look," he grumped. "Just look at the prickly pear—"

"Guys," Lani interrupted. "Can we get on with it?"

"Sure enough, baby," Scott answered. "Hey, if there's anything going on, I'll capture it on video for both of you so you can enjoy it with popcorn later." He dropped his pack to the ground and undid the zipper that ran from the base to the top. A smart phone appeared in his hand a moment later.

"You're gonna call somebody?"

"Nope, Rollo. Video." Scott tapped at the phone, then swung it around. He briefly pointed the tiny lens on the back toward Rollo. The older man leaned forward to watch the playback of what had just been recorded.

"If you'd venture out of the 19th century from time to time, you'd know that phones these days can take pictures and video. I can even post it online from here."

He peered at the phone and grimaced.

"Well, I *could* if there was any service out here."

Rollo ignored the dig and whistled appreciatively.

"Pretty cool."

"Yep. Lani and I have found some uses for it." A big grin played across Scott's face.

Lani colored and slammed her elbow into Scott's ribs, but she wore a smirk of her own.

"Oh," Rollo said. "That *is* handy. I'll be damned."

Moments later, Scott slipped through the tall grass, his head down in an almost unconscious effort to keep it from bobbing above the high ground ahead and revealing his presence.

What am I doing, he asked himself. It's not stalking. It's certainly not creeping. Skulking, he decided. I'm skulking toward the enemy. Assuming that they are the enemy, that is.

Which raised another interesting question. Who was up ahead? Were they Rollo's Forest Service pyromaniacs? Scott didn't share his buddy's conspiracy theories, but not because of any inherent respect for government employees. To the contrary, he considered anybody who preferred a life of administering laws and rules and living off of taxes to one of persuading people to buy what you had to sell and living on what you could earn to be more worthy of contempt than fear.

To a large extent, he'd always had a gut-level revulsion toward authority. The idea that some people claimed a "right" to boss other people around at the point of a gun, even if only implied, just struck him as absurd.

Then, years of writing about business had crystallized his convictions. So far as he could tell, government regulators were good primarily at tripping up the competent and propping up the screw-ups. Especially if the screw-ups were their buddies.

Different agencies had slightly different cultures, but it was like choosing from a menu of bloody-minded dysfunction and self-importance.

His musings had to share brainpower with his concern for the terrain. The grass through which he ... skulked ... scratched his bare legs below his shorts and caught in his hiking socks.

As he approached the ridgeline, he dropped to his hands and knees and began crawling through the grass, the phone clamped in his right hand. He grimaced as his knees scraped along the ground.

The air carried the sweet smell of ponderosa pines, a hint of dust suspended on the wind—and a strong whiff of gasoline.

He flopped on his belly and wriggled up the hump for a look

to the other side.

What the fuck?

Five, no, six people were in a circle wearing the bottom halves of Forest Service uniforms. Two of the men in the circle looked like unhappy cops at the beach, with short hair, aviator shades and deep scowls to accessorize their semi-undress.

Two of the bare-chested rangers were women, and they clearly weren't believers in brassieres. The one with curly reddish hair was even worth a second look.

The six rangers surrounded a seventh ranger who stood at their center with a lit match cupped in his hand.

Scott remembered to tap the shutter "button" on his phone, and held it above the grass to record the doings below.

It's stranger than Rollo knows, Scott thought. The rangers sealed off the area so they could hold some twisted pagan ritual in the middle of nowhere. Jesus Christ, what if they decide to hold a human sacrifice?

He missed the comforting weight of his gun, left behind with Rollo and Lani.

One of the women rangers—the one with chopped, dark hair—turned from the circle, lit torch held forward, and began passing through the grass, setting it aflame. She paused, dropped the torch in the grass, and donned a yellow coat from a pile of similar garments near one of the trucks.

"Not so close," the one with the matches yelled. "Take it further out, damn it. Burn the forest, not us!"

Scott hoped the phone's microphone had caught those words. He slowly panned the camera toward the San Francisco peaks towering above Flagstaff in the distance, then back to the firebug jamboree in the grassy field ahead.

Just as he carefully peered up to make sure the phone was capturing what he intended, a sensation like that of an oversized slug curling up in his right ear for a nap diverted his attention from the fiery festivities. Lying on his belly, observing nefarious doings in the forest, fifteen miles from paved road, Scott had received a wet willy.

"Shit," Scott yelped, slapping his hand to his ear.

He rolled on his back to find the source of the unexpected offense—and stared straight up into the grinning face of Champ. Left ear pointed to the sky, right ear folded in a salute, slobber dripping from the tongue that had just probed the man's ear, the dog panted, and then licked his face in canine adoration. His leash hung unattended from his collar.

Scott tilted his head, briefly, toward his friends. Lani had her arms stretched out toward him. She tilted her head and silently mouthed the word "sorry." Rollo's pack was open in front of him and he was frantically fiddling with something he'd apparently pulled from the interior.

Remembering where he was, Scott tilted his head back for an upside-down view of the half-dressed firebugs. The first thing he noticed was that the group he'd been watching was now watching him. One of two rangers with matching crew cuts and shades approached. His scowl was even deeper than before and he had a compact gun in his hand that Scott recognized as a Sig.

Is it a 9mm? Maybe it's a .40. Then it occurred to him that there were better things to worry about.

Scott slowly rolled over, and then rose to his feet with his hands raised high—the smart phone exposed for everybody to see.

"Hey folks. You must be ..." He surveyed the gestating inferno in front of him. "... State Department? Anybody have a light?"

Chapter 18

H is nerves sizzling with adrenaline rush, Jason watched Ray stalk forward toward the stranger and his dog. He was surprised to see the wanna-be G-man draw a gun from a hip holster. So was Tim, apparently, who looked at his partner's pistol with open envy, and absent-mindedly stroked at his own hip. The group was well-armed, but most of the weapons were in the trucks as befit their just-in-case status.

Jason missed the stranger's opening comment, but it was obviously a wisecrack, to judge by Terry's snort and the snarls emanating from Ray and Tim.

"Buddy, you're in trouble," Ray said. "This area is closed to the public for your own safety. You're not supposed to be here."

The stranger didn't look impressed. While his hands were up in a gesture of surrender, his face under his ball cap and beneath his sunglasses revealed a barely suppressed smirk. He faced the rangers, medium height and lean in a safari-style shirt with the sleeves rolled up and buttoned in place. But his legs below his shorts looked poised to bolt at a moment's notice.

Ray must have picked up on the stranger's disdain. Jason's ear's rang as the wanna-be cop fired a shot in the air, and he could barely make out the following words.

"Goddamnit! I'm talking to you!"

The stranger's dog, a big, black-and-white Australian shepherd mix, obviously picked up on the confrontational vibe; happily licking his master's face just a moment before, now he glared at Ray and growled.

Jason took a quick glance at his team, and honestly couldn't blame the stranger for his attitude. Bare-chested, bare-breasted and brandishing flaming torches, the gathering looked like... Hell, Jason didn't know what it looked like, but he suddenly felt like he should have a bone through his nose. The stranger looked too comfortable with the outdoors to be persuaded that this was an official Forest Service operation.

"Crap. Ray, grab that guy and bring him over here. Let's see what's on his phone."

That's when the popping noises sounded—one, two, three. And three little spurts of dirt erupted in front of Ray.

Tim and Ray immediately hit the dirt. Jason stared at Samantha, who looked at Rena, who peered at Bob, who glanced at Terry. Terry shielded his eyes with his left hand and pointed off into the trees at the far side of the field.

"Hey, somebody over there is shooting at us!"

Two more pops.

Everybody joined Ray and Tim in the dirt.

Chapter 19

Phone in hand, Scott ran like hell back to his friends. He raced across the field, panting and sweating from nerves as much as from exertion. Champ trotted easily alongside with his mouth open in a big grin.

The dog had no idea what was going on—he just knew his human friend had involved him in an adventure, and he was having fun.

Lani threw Scott's pack at him as he reached the trees. The pack's blue-gray fabric and yellow bungee cords filled his vision until he caught it one-handed in mid-air and hung a strap over his left shoulder with barely a break in stride. He felt the heavy weight of his gun in its holster slap him in the small of the back, and he vowed never again to leave it behind.

Lani ran ahead of him, runner's legs pumping, long, blonde hair flying from under her floppy trail hat, and athletic bra straining to do its duty.

Already huffing, Rollo took the lead. He had his pack over one shoulder, and what looked like an undersized rifle bobbed in his free hand.

They ran through the woods, breathing deeply the thick, sweet smell of the trees that was now flavored with a strong hint of smoke. They ran between trees, across a bed of pine needles, and through high foxtails that stuck in their socks, pierced their ankles and caused Champ to yelp.

And they ran without direction, because panic erased whatever vestigial hunch as to the truck's location they might have retained.

They came out of the trees and ran along a dirt road, preferring a clear path to somewhere over a blind run through forest that might bring them back to the firebugs—the *armed* firebugs.

They ran until Rollo stopped in his tracks, pivoted to face back the way they'd come, and flopped into a sitting position with his back against a tree. His hat slid back on his head and a spray of graying hair escaped to form an off-color halo around his head. He gasped for breath.

"Can't– Can't– Can't–"

He held the mini-rifle pointed straight ahead.

Scott dropped his own pack and drew his pistol, releasing the thumb safety as he palmed the gun.

"What the fuck was that?" he said when he'd caught his breath. He tried to listen for the sound of runners or vehicles in pursuit, but the way the three were breathing a helicopter could have flown overhead and escaped detection.

"Maybe they're really pissed about the truck," Rollo wheezed. He managed a chuckle that dissolved into a cough to let them know he was joking.

"They *shot* at you," Lani finally said. She turned to face Rollo. "And then *you* shot back."

Rollo rolled his eyes.

"They just fired a warning shot, Lani."

Scott nodded.

"And Rollo just got them to keep their heads down. Nobody actually got hit."

Lani just stared, and patted absently at Champ, who leaned against her leg.

"So it was all in good fun?" Her face flushed bright red beneath her suntan.

Scott smiled.

"Well, maybe not 'fun.'"

He turned his attention to Rollo.

"Is that your Erector-set rifle?"

Rollo grinned.

"I always carry this in my pack. It's my good luck charm."

Rollo unscrewed a nut at the base of the rifle's pistol grip, which was a molded extrusion of the black, plastic stock, and then he separated the receiver from the stock. "The barrel comes off, too, and everything stashes inside the stock. It's one of my favorite toys."

"I like it. But why didn't you grab my pistol instead of putting together your little MacGyver gadget?"

"Hell, Scott. I've never shot your pistol. I figured it'd be faster to put this thing together than to figure out that IQ test you call a gun."

Lani pressed the heels of her hands to her forehead and let out a sigh.

"Guys, I'm so happy you're having a bonding moment, but what do we do next?"

There was a long moment of silence.

"I mean, bizarre as it is, Rollo was apparently right about rangers setting the forest on fire. And now they're after—" Her voice broke.

After a moment, she spoke, her voice once again clear and strong.

"Basically, we're fucked."

Scott reached around the slim blonde, and then dramatically twirled her into his arms and planted a kiss on her lips.

"But baby, this is your opportunity to see me in action. You can witness my grace under fire—"

"Witness you run your ass off under fire, more like," Rollo offered.

Scott ignored him.

"This is a chance for genuine heroics, honey."

"Oh shit. I hope you're not serious."

Scott gently returned Lani to her feet.

"Not completely. But I thought it might cheer you up. Anyway, if I'm not gonna look dashing now, I'll never have a chance."

He shot his girlfriend what he hoped was a reassuring smile. Then he looked ahead along the rutted track through the forest.

"Hey, where do you think this road goes?"

Chapter 20

With smoke wreathed around his head, Jason barely suppressed a dry cough. He shot a glance down the road toward the spot where they'd seen the stranger—and been shot at by *somebody*. Fire was spreading at that site, the smoke was getting thicker and he and his friends were very obviously not the only people roaming the woods with guns.

He wanted to go home.

But Van Kamp had other ideas.

"Get that son of a bitch," the diminutive uber-ranger had ordered him via two-way radio. It was an impressive device—larger than usual and, importantly, supposedly secure from eavesdropping. Jason could visualize the little man standing on his chair and leaning over his desk with spittle flying from between his gnashing teeth. He shuddered.

"Get that SOB, and get whoever his friends are. We can't have them peddling photographs of you setting a fire."

"But they *shot* at us!"

"That's right! And we can't let that kind of disdain for Forest Service personnel—well, people who *look* like Forest Service personnel—go unpunished."

So here he hunched over the hood of his truck, with a fire

creeping close enough to (he shot another look over his shoulder) slow-roast his backside. He smoothed the map with his hands, and traced the outline of a road.

"This is where we are, along FR 538. The people we saw ran off in this direction, which leads further back into the forest, toward the rim."

Tim stabbed at a spot on the map with a finger grubby from gasoline and soot. He and Ray had lingered too long near the flames, torn between desire to race off after the strangers, and fear of being trapped between firearms and fire. The result was a pinkish glow, like that of pork on its way to barbecued perfection.

"It looks like 538 links up with 231—whaddya call it ... Woody Mountain Road—up ahead."

"Yes," Jason answered. "There's a connecting road several miles down that brings you back to 231."

"So if we grab those people fast enough, we can get around the fire before it cuts us off?"

"If we drive fast enough—and if the fire doesn't move too fast."

"How are we going to fit everybody in the trucks?" Rena asked. "I mean, we can get one or two in easy, but can we really jam several prisoners in with us and still control them?"

Terry looked on with a faint smile on his face, and Jason could guess his colleague's thoughts. Squat and muscular—the opposite of Terry in almost every way—her bare torso covered in a layer of dirt and soot like an Amazon warrior painted for battle, Rena looked like she could put any two prisoners in a headlock without much difficulty.

But Jason didn't say a word in response; he just returned his eyes to the map. Even Rena's friend Bob kept his eyes on his shoes. The Floral Supremacy people were full partners in (Jason whispered the name to himself) the Carthage Option; they should know what was expected.

Rena looked from face to face, awaiting an answer to her question.

Finally, Tim turned and snarled, "We ain't bringin' 'em back."

Rena mouthed a silent "Oh."

"So what's down that way, anyway?" Ray asked. "Where are these people headed?"

Terry, who knew the area best, spoke up. "Way down the road, 538 eventually ends at the Casner Mountain trailhead. That splits off into two trails. One of them heads into Sycamore Canyon; the other leaves off in the middle of nowhere—down dirt road, miles from Highway 89A.

"If they're smart, though, they'll duck down 538E."

"Why's that," Ray asked.

"That road leads to Dorsey Spring trail and Kelsey Spring trail, and both of those take you down to Geronimo Spring in Sycamore Canyon."

"Does Sycamore Canyon get them anywhere?"

"If they follow it all the way down, it takes them to a pretty busy trailhead. From there they could catch a ride to Clarkdale."

"Fuck. Is there water along there?"

"Some. Especially with the rains at this time of year."

"Fuck."

Jason sighed. "All right, folks. Let's get in the trucks and see if we can't catch these people before they get into the canyon."

Five minutes later, with dust and smoke mingling in the air behind the vehicles, they approached the intersection of forest Roads 538 and 538E.

Then the engine in Jason's truck sputtered and stopped.

Tim pulled his truck along side Jason's. From the driver's side he called across his cab, "What in Hell is wrong now?"

Then the second engine sputtered and stopped.

Jason tapped gently on his now-useless steering wheel. He watched the dust settle around the truck. Then he turned to Samantha, sitting in the shotgun seat with a look of concern on her face.

"Out of curiosity, just how much gasoline did you siphon from the truck tanks?"

Chapter 21

V an Kamp wound up as if to pitch his two-way radio across the
small motel room, then thought better of it. It was official-
issue, after all, even if his possession and use of it was a bit
*un*official, and a fastball pitch through the room's television set
would likely take a fair chunk out of his paycheck. Instead, he
carefully dropped the gadget onto the bed. That paycheck was likely
to grow in the near future, to compensate for a host of eagerly
anticipated new responsibilities. How could the administrator of a
vast wilderness too flammable for human habitation be expected to
survive on the pittance he took home?

But, for now, that pittance was all he had, so onto the bed the
radio must go.

His aborted wind-up didn't go unnoticed.

"Bad news?" the Park Service man asked. He sat by the
room's open window, catching the summer breeze that carried the
noises and odors of busy Route 66. With storm clouds moving in,
the temperature had dropped enough that nobody in the room felt
obligated to demand air conditioning. Still, the room was close and
stale-smelling, and fresh air was welcome.

Van Kamp didn't answer immediately. The pint-sized ranger
paced the small room, coming face to shirt button with first

Greenfield, then the BLM official. The reminder of small stature put him in an even fouler mood.

"Goddamn yes. That idiot managed to run out of gas. His trucks are stranded in the middle of the forest, which means they're toast if that fire they set does what it's supposed to do. That's *three* trucks he's lost. Three!"

Greenfield glared at him from across the room. He wore the same shirt and sports jacket he'd had on earlier. In fact, it was the only clothing Van Kamp had ever seen him in. Which fact went a long way toward explaining the stale air in the room.

"That fire *better* do what it's supposed to do. Those trees must die for a cause." His voice rumbled like thunder. His beard trembled ever so slightly. "I won't let their deaths be in vain." He drew out the word "vain," adding at least one extra syllable.

"Jesus, you're good at that," the Park Service man said. "We have to get you on TV again."

Greenfield blinked, then smiled.

"Anyway," the BLM official broke in, shooting a skeptical glance at Greenfield. "At least the fire got started. That's what we wanted. "Once the hotshots are committed to suppressing the fire, I can have my people get started on Fredonia and Kanab. We'll get the firefighting resources spread a little thin."

Van Kamp sighed.

"Yes, but that id—" He stopped himself. "Jason is out there chasing witnesses now—witnesses who shot at him. With the hotshots in place, we really can't send anybody in to help him. We'll have to count on the team we have in place to get the job done."

The Park Service man pursed his lips, then looked at Greenfield.

"Are your people up to that? I mean, are they up to a gun fight in the desert?"

Greenfield folded his hands in front of his chest.

"Oh yes. All three of them are tough as nails. And Bob once shot up a landscaper's office."

"What?"

"Well, it's just cruel, you know. Landscapers mutilate our friends. Bob takes great exception to that."

Chapter 22

"Kelsey Spring it is, then," Scott said, looking at the rustic trail marker at the end of the rocky, rutted road. "Does anybody know where this trail takes us?"

Lani dropped her pack to the ground, unzipped the lid pocket and fished a dog-eared trail guide from inside. She sat cross-legged on the ground, into which her dust-coated legs seemed to blend.

"Does this take us down into the canyon?" Rollo asked. He hunched down to look at the trail entry. His bulk loomed over that of the small blonde, and she leaned slightly to her left to open the distance between them.

"Which canyon?" Scott asked. He scratched absent-mindedly behind Champ's ears, while the dog leaned against his knees.

"*My* canyon," Rollo answered. "Sycamore. I've been stomping through there for years. I even have some stuff cached up on Packard Mesa above the canyon."

He cocked his head to the side.

"Well, I might. I stashed it there a while ago. I can be forgetful sometimes."

Lani ran her finger down a page in the book.

"It looks like the trail branches off. We could loop back up the Dorsey trail and maybe get behind them."

Scott glanced down the road behind them, then at the sky above. It was rapidly filling with smoke, which rose into the sky to blend with an oncoming wall of clouds.

"I don't think so."

"Uh uh," Rollo echoed, following Scott's gaze.

"Well ... yeah, it does also go down into the canyon. There's water along the way, too."

"Sounds like a plan," Scott said. He gave Champ a last pat, then stepped toward the trailhead.

Lani didn't budge. She sat in place, trail guide in her hand, her eyes focused on nothing in particular.

Scott stopped in place. He took a sip from his drinking tube, cleared his throat, and then scuffed the ground with the toe of his hiking shoe.

"Is that all right with you?"

"No."

Rollo strolled past the trailhead, and then paused.

"I'll be ..." He pointed vaguely down the trail. Then he followed his finger and disappeared.

"So?"

"This is nuts." Lani stared up at him. Her legs were uncrossed and splayed wide across the dirt. "I'm a schoolteacher. You're an unemployed editor who just *hates* being told what to do. Rollo's an ... I don't know what the hell he is."

"A free spirit," yelled a voice from down the trail. "I'm a free spirit."

"You're a bum," Scott answered. "But I like you anyway."

"But that's all we are," Lani continued. "Who are we to go around out here shooting at pyromaniac forest rangers and then run off into the desert?"

"Oh shit. Is she getting all existential?"

"Shut up, Rollo."

Scott dropped to one knee and took Lani's hand in his own. He gently kissed the back of her hand.

"First of all, I'm not much of an editor. I haven't done much editing in a long time. Mostly, I'm a loafer who likes to hike and shoot and cash paychecks from companies that haven't yet realized that they no longer need my services."

Lani smiled and shook her head.

"I hope that makes you feel better."

"Not really."

"Well, how's this. We're the people on the spot. And if we don't get moving, I strongly suspect the bad guys will catch up with us. And that would be bad. Work for you?"

Lani sighed.

Scott rose and extended a hand to help his girlfriend to her feet. Then he kissed her.

"I love you. Remember that."

"I remember. And I love you."

A rustling came from the direction of the trailhead.

"Well, I don't love either of you. So can we get going before somebody sets fire to us?"

Scott looked at Lani; he cocked an eyebrow in a silent question. She nodded in response. They strolled silently to the rim of the canyon just yards from the trailhead and took a last look at the gouge in the Earth they hoped would provide refuge. Light played across the rocks and trees below. A slow rumble of thunder echoed from the canyon walls.

"I hope you have some food in that cache of yours," Lani called out.

The older man answered without turning around.

"I hope I don't. You have no idea how long it's been since I put it there."

Kelsey Trail isn't a shy trail; it runs hikers through a series of steep switchbacks that has the leader of any trek catching loose pocket change dropped by members of the party behind him.

Forest crowded the trio and the steep trail required attention, so the world closed in to become a circle encompassing three people and one dog. Rocks rolled underfoot, dirt-hard-packed from the tramping of boots and the glare of the sun caused lugged soles to skid and bushes—sharp Arizona bushes with pointy Arizona thorns—reached out to snare fabric and scrape skin.

The circle filled with the sound of wind rustling through branches, heavy breathing from hikers intent on keeping their footing, slurps as Scott and Lani sipped from their drinking tubes and Rollo gulped water from an ancient but still-serviceable soda bottle.

And there was also the happy snuffling and snorting of a dog overjoyed to explore the multitude of smells to be found along the trail—and to make friends with the wildlife.

"Goddamnit, Champ!" Lani yelled. "Leave that rabbit alone!"

Kelsey Spring itself appeared after half-a-mile. On a welcome shelf of flat land, and just a short jog to the right of the trail, water flowed from a pipe into a battered metal trough.

"Anybody need water?" Scott asked.

Nobody answered, so on Scott, Rollo and Champ went — until they realized they were missing a trail companion. They retraced their steps a hundred feet or so to the spring, where Lani squatted, sifting through the contents of her backpack. Her hand reappeared from the pack's depths, clutching a bright-red parcel emblazoned with a white cross.

"What're you doing, hon?"

Lani produced a rolled-up sandwich baggy filled with white, powdery crystals.

"Oh, no," Rollo said. "This ain't no 'Bright Lights, Big City' re-enactment."

Lani ignored him.

"Baby, aren't epsom salts a laxative?"

"Yeah."

Lani gestured at the water tank.

Scott smiled.

"Oh. Hell, why not? Is there anything else we can use?"

Rollo's mouth opened in a wide O. He dropped his pack to the ground and fished inside a side pocket. He produced a small cardboard box.

Scott looked at the box quizzically.

Rollo shrugged.

"All that jerky I eat can be a little binding, if you know what I mean."

Scott ripped into the box and handed the contents to Lani, who added it to the soup she'd already made of the Epsom salts in the steel trough. She gave the mess a stir with a stick.

"Looks good to me."

And off they went again.

They hiked to the Babe's Hole spring where hills clustered to shelter a plank-covered well from which water flowed into a bubbling pool of water. Sadly out of adulterants to add to the water supply, they passed on by.

Ponderosa pine soon gave way to oak and sycamore trees, and the temperature inched upwards.

At a trail junction, they spurned the left-hand fork that would take them back up to the rim where lurked fire and firebugs, and chose instead the trail to Geronimo Spring at the bottom of Sycamore Canyon.

Time passed. The trail grew harsher and treacherous rocks threatened to send the hikers tumbling downward to their destination faster than planned.

Soon, though, the trail ended at a shady, tree-lined trail intersection where Little LO Canyon opened into Sycamore Canyon. High rock walls towered above. A left-hand turn led to the spring and the big canyon beyond.

Lani was the first of the trio to take advantage of Geronimo Spring, though Champ jumped the line to lap water from the wooden trough. The thin blonde filled her water bladder and extra bottles while Rollo waited his turn and Scott mixed up batches of an oily yellow solution from two small squeeze bottles of chemicals. He dumped the stuff into each water container Lani handed him.

Rollo snorted.

"Ya gotta toughen up your guts so the water cooties leave you alone."

Scott didn't look up.

"I have no doubt the parasites have more to fear from you than you have to fear from parasites."

Light dimmed in the canyon and a spattering of rain polka-dotted the rocks.

Scott lifted his hand, palm upward.

"We're gonna get wet."

He turned and looked back the way they'd come.

"D'ya think they're still behind us?"

Rollo shrugged.

"Probably. I have a strong feeling they're a little ticked off about the visit we paid them."

He shrugged.

"I just hope they're not too much better prepared than we are for this little adventure."

Chapter 23

"OK. So, does anybody else have a rain jacket?" Nobody responded, leaving Terry as the only member of the group with his hand in the air. After a quick glance around his ring of teammates, he dropped it to his side.

"I think Tim has a poncho," Terry finally offered.

Jason just glared in response; the comment didn't deserve anything else.

"Well, that's a big help," Ray barked. "Maybe he can use it to protect himself from the fire. You know, instead of the Nomex coats that *somebody* left back in the forest."

Jason flushed. He wasn't entirely sure that leaving their fire-resistant gear in a neat pile near the spot where they'd encountered the stranger was entirely his fault, but he was in charge. Well, sort of. He was the one taking the blame anyway.

Ray seemed to stare wistfully down the road in the direction Tim had disappeared to meet up with a truck and equipment sent by Van Kamp and Greenfield. Terry, Bob and Rena's gaze followed. Jason was happy to note that Samantha's eyes stayed on him.

"Well, what's done is done. Tim is on his way to the mouth of Sycamore Canyon. He'll head off the people ahead of us in case we can't catch up with them."

After a pause, he added, "I'm sure he'll be just fine."

Ray muttered something.

"What's that?"

"I said we should have given him some barbecue sauce."

Jason's lips tightened, but he didn't bother answering. Instead, he hoisted his daypack to his back and made a show of buckling the sternum strap that kept the shoulder straps from slipping too far apart. The light pack settled into place easily—a testament to the small load he'd packed in anticipation of a casual day of pyromania. Then he lifted his rifle from the ground, feeling a little off-balance from the unaccustomed weight of the M-16 gripped in his right hand.

"All right people. The tracks go in this direction. So let's get going." He stepped toward the Kelsey trailhead.

Following his lead, the others donned their own packs and lifted the weapons they'd off-loaded from the trucks before abandoning the vehicles and their empty gas tanks to the advancing fire.

Hanging back so he could bring up the rear, Ray grabbed the rifle from Rena's hands and gave it a quick inspection.

"You sure you know how to use this?"

Rena glared at the crew-cut park ranger, then abruptly grabbed at the rifle. Ray dug in his heels and pulled back. A silent tug-of-war ensued, punctuated by soft grunts. His boots leaving visible tracks in the dirt, the ranger lost ground inch by inch.

"Hey man," Bob said, stepping between the antagonists. "Leave her alone." The wispy beard dangling from his chin wagged as he spoke.

Ray glared at the floral supremacist—a wasted gesture with his eyes hidden behind his shades.

"No, really. I think she can take you. And she's good with that rifle."

Ray let go of the rifle, sending Rena sprawling in the dirt. He flexed his fingers to pump blood back into the strained digits.

"Good with a rifle? Where in hell did she learn to operate an M-16?"

"Everybody at the Center gets weapons training. It's part of why we were assigned to the team."

"No shit?"

Rena rose from the ground with the gun in hand. She brushed dust from her breasts and shorts with her free hand.

"I practice all the time," she said, spitting the words along with a few pine needles.

"On what?"

"Cattle mostly. Sometimes SUV dealerships or–"

Ray tugged his sunglasses down his nose and peered at the squat environmentalist with unobstructed eyes.

"You shoot *cows*?"

Rena sniffed and turned away.

"Hey man," Bob whispered. "They eat those beautiful desert plants."

"We usually use AK-47s, though," Rena added. "They're a lot tougher than these plastic toys."

Ray gaped.

"Oh, that'd be easy to explain," Terry commented. "Federal forest rangers armed with Russian surplus weapons."

"Well … maybe," Rena said. "But the AKs are a lot easier to maintain. I can field-strip one in the dark."

Far ahead and entirely oblivious to the tumult at the rear of his column, Jason stopped in his tracks along the trail and held up his hand.

"What's wrong," Samantha asked. She reached her hand out and brushed Jason's bare shoulder.

"Um … uh …" the team leader stuttered, momentarily

distracted. He stared into the woman's eyes. Bambi, he thought. Just like Bambi.

"Is something wrong?" Samantha repeated.

Jason shook his head.

"No, but I heard something. It sounded like somebody yelling 'Champ'. Who in Hell is a champ?"

Chapter 24

With the red nylon pouches of his doggie backpack flapping against his furry flanks, the black-and-white beast launched himself at a large boulder along the rock-strewn floor of the canyon. His paws splayed in four directions, the animal tightly gripped the steep rock surface. The tips of his claws extended into any cracks or crevice that could provide support. With a sudden heave, he hopped forward, set his grip again, and then pulled himself to the top. Eyes wide, panting and grinning, the dog stood atop the boulder, gazing down the canyon. He turned to gaze at his companions, his tail wagging wildly in celebration.

"Goddamnit, Champ," Lani yelled. "Get down from there!"

"Is that his full name?"

Lani glanced at Rollo, then continued walking down-canyon, away from Geronimo Spring and the trail from the rim.

"What?"

"Is Goddamnit Champ the dog's formal name? I mean you always say those words together when you're pissed at the dog. I figure it's like some moms who address their kids informally—like calling a boy 'Johnny'—then get all formal when the kids step out of line." He cupped his hand to his bearded mouth and called out, "Oh, J-o-o-o-n-a-th-a-a-a-n!"

Lani stared.

"I can't tell whether you're serious or not."

Scott sighed.

"He's just needling you, hon."

Rollo chuckled.

"Well, you do treat that dog like a baby."

Lani shot a look at her boyfriend. She smiled.

"Well, Scott does call Champ our baby substitute."

"Oh *really?*"

"Oh crap."

"That's adorable."

"Leave it alone, Rollo."

Serenaded by chorus of chuckles shared all around, the three stepped slowly and carefully along the floor of the canyon. They stepped over rocks when possible, and hopped from one to another when it wasn't.

The spatter of raindrops picked up in frequency, now landing faster than the wet freckles they left could evaporate from rock and dirt. Scott glanced up just as the canyon lit up with a bright flash. Moments later, a dull boom echoed through the rocky corridor.

Without a word, he dropped his pack to the ground, and fished out a small, tightly stuffed nylon bag. From this he quickly extracted a rain jacket. As he cinched the zipper under his chin, he looked up to see Lani shrugging into her own jacket. Rollo patiently stood in place, already hidden under a voluminous poncho that fit over his head, body and pack like a dirt-encrusted mumu.

The older man snorted.

"You're gonna sweat like a pig in that thing," he warned, pointing at the jacket. "You'd stay dryer in the rain than you will in that sauna suit."

Scott flamboyantly reached under each of his arms to unzip

vents and let the air circulate.

"Oooh. Fancy."

Lani glanced back the way they'd come.

"We should probably get going. I don't know if we're being followed, but I don't want them catching up with us."

"We're being followed," Rollo said. "There's no way they can let us get away with that video that Scott took."

Scott fired off a sharp look.

"I hope you're not trying to lay this on my shoulders. You were pretty enthusiastic about playing junior detective, if I remember right."

"Nope. Just stating a fact. They're after us."

The three walked in silence for several minutes, while the fourth member of the group scouted ahead for hostile rabbits.

"So," Lani broke in. "What are we going to do with that video? Is it worth all this trouble?"

"Damned if I know if it's worth it," Scott answered. "But since we're going to take heat for having the thing, we might as well do something with it."

"We gonna get those bastards?" Rollo asked.

"Maybe."

Scott suddenly stumbled and stubbed his toe against a boulder, the pain penetrating the rubber bumper on the light-hiking shoe. He unleashed a steady stream of profanity as he hopped on his undamaged foot, clutching at the offended limb.

Lani bent to examine the injured toe. She clutched helpfully at the foot, cradling it in order to administer any necessary medical attention. In imminent danger of losing his balance on the wet rocks, Scott finally waved her off.

"Are you OK?"

Scott cursed once more, and then set his foot back down on the ground.

"I will be."

Rollo looked on, smirking.

"Oh you kids and your crazy dances."

Scott unleashed another round of profanity.

"Was that French? I'm pretty sure that was something filthy in French."

"Italian," Scott snapped. "I can offend in four languages."

The trio continued down the canyon, Lani giving Scott's foot an occasional look of concern. Scott responded by deliberately compensating for the ache in his toe, so that his limp became a strut.

"Are you sure you're OK?"

"I'm fine."

Rollo cleared his throat.

"So, you said 'maybe'?"

"What?"

"You said 'maybe' we could get these bastards."

"Oh yeah. Well, one of the things I did for my late, unlamented employer was maintain a distribution list for press releases. When I wanted to try to scare up a press mention about a conference or an article, I'd cook up a press release with our PR flacks and fire it off to the list. It'd automatically get sent to a couple of hundred tech reporters."

Lani shot him a glance.

"Could we send the video–?"

"Nope. It's only set up for text messages. But if we can get in range of a cell tower, I can upload the video to YouTube. Then we can send out an e-mail press release pointing a few hundred journalists to the thing."

Rollo paused, and then squinted at Scott through the rain. Water rolled off the brim of his hat and streamed from his poncho.

"I thought you got fired. Isn't that gonna crimp your plans to use the company press list?"

"Maybe."

"Maybe again!"

"Maybe, I said. But I doubt it. I worked there for a long time, and I gave myself a few extra passwords while I had the opportunity. And they've always been slow about deleting accounts and enforcing basic security. They don't do any of the things our articles advised our readers to do."

Rollo turned his face back down the canyon.

"So ... maybe we'll be able to show that video clip to a bunch of geeks who might not know what to make of it anyway."

"Maybe so."

"You have any other ideas?"

Scott looked at the sky. A flash of lightning lit his face, and the roar of thunder crashed from the canyon walls.

"Yep. I'm thinking that we're walking in a dry streambed in a rainstorm. Maybe that's not a good idea. Let's find a place to hole up."

Chapter 25

Tim fumed, building a head of steam with every step he took away from Jason and the rest of the crew. He stalked toward his rendezvous with a Forest Service truck somewhere along Woody Mountain Road—where, exactly, depended on how fast he walked and how hard the driver stood on the gas pedal. He stepped along briskly, with the fire behind him, though he felt little cause for concern. The wind had died down and the rain put a literal damper on the fiery festivities.

The weather pissed him off. They'd planned on high winds and dry air to do most of their work for them, but nature had something else up its sleeve. The fire should have been roaring out of control by now, consuming dry duff and beetle-damaged ponderosa pines in wholesale lots. Instead, it sputtered along. The blaze was less of a raging inferno, than a cozy weenie roast.

Speaking of weenies ... Jason pissed him off. That little weirdo couldn't organize a Girl Scout outing. How do you forget drip torches? How do you abandon your protective gear? How do you get yourself photographed by some random wanderer at the ass-end of a sealed-off road?

And whatever was developing between the team leader and that strange plant-freak girl couldn't be good news.

But most of all, the strangers pissed him off. First and

foremost, Tim considered himself a law-enforcement officer—an agent of official policy and defender of order. You do *not* spy on law enforcement officers. Sneaking around in the brush with a smart phone suggested an unseemly distrust of officialdom.

And you certainly don't *shoot* at law enforcement officers. That leads to anarchy. And Tim wasn't about to let anarchy gain the upper hand.

Tim felt the weight of his gun on his hip—his official, Park Service-issued gun, and he felt the weight of the Park Service in the weight of that gun, and the weight of the government behind the Park Service. The more Tim thought about the situation, the more he determined to set things right, once and for all.

Step by muddy step, water seeped into Tim's shoes, soaked his shorts, dripped from his short-cropped hair and fogged his sunglasses. And all of that pissed him off too.

Eventually, a pair of headlights turned into a Forest Service truck. Tim stepped forward, pulled the door open, and thrust his head inside.

"Not happy! I'm *definitely* not happy."

The driver gaped. Only then did Tim recognize Van Kamp himself at the wheel, sitting far forward to reach the vehicle controls. Two BLM rangers filled the back seat, apparently along as muscle for the pint-sized conspirator.

"Ranger Vasquez? Is that you?"

"Who else? Sir."

"Do you need medical attention? Food?"

"I just need an overnight pack and ammunition. Lots of ammunition." He looked at the BLM men in the back of the truck. One of them gulped and a bead of sweat fell from his brow to his collar.

"Oh, and a new shirt."

Chapter 26

Van Kamp's nerves were well and truly frayed by the time he arrived back at the district headquarters. Assisted by the persuasive powers of the BLM rangers—one of whom now nursed a wrenched shoulder and threatened to file a worker's compensation claim—Van Kamp had convinced Tim to delay his return to the chase for a day. That gave the park ranger a night to rest and, more importantly, cool off before interacting once again with the public.

Soles thumping against the scuffed linoleum floor of the hallway leading to his office, Van Kamp thought troubled thoughts as he watched his shoes and pushed his way past the door to his office—then bumped head-first into a sports jacket in need of a good dry-cleaning.

"Christ! How the hell did you get in here?"

"Your staff let me in," Greenfield boomed. He stepped back from the doorway, sat in the chair opposite the desk—the very chair in which Van Kamp habitually terrorized any subordinate who displeased him—and crossed his hands over his belly. "I haven't had any word from my people and I want to see if you have any news."

Van Kamp uttered a string of obscenities, then slipped behind his desk and climbed into his chair.

"They let you in?"

"Well, they've seen me with you."

Van Kamp grimaced.

"They've seen me with the plumber, too. That doesn't mean they should serve him coffee and cookies in my office."

Greenfield smiled, a little hesitantly.

"Bottled water and a turkey sandwich, actually." The big-screen, biblical-epic voice managed to sound almost apologetic. "So, have you heard from them?"

Van Kamp stared, while considering whether to throw a temper tantrum. After a moment, he choked down his anger.

"Not from them, but from one of the Park Service people on the team."

"Not one of those flat-head, wannabe—"

"Yep. One of them. The Park Service takes its law enforcement duties ve-e-e-ry seriously. I'm told that the fire is set, but there's trouble—the job was half-botched and they were photographed in the act."

Greenfield grumbled and sat deeper in his chair. He sank even further into his clothes, seeming to disappear into his jacket and wrinkled shirt as Van Kamp repeated the tale he'd heard from Ranger Tim Vasquez.

"I'm thinking maybe we should wait and see what happens in Sycamore Canyon before be move forward. We can send more people in to find the witnesses—people who aren't complete fuck-ups. When things settle down, we'll get back to business."

Greenfield stirred. His bearded chin rose from his chest. His eyes flashed and met those of Van Kamp, seeming to bore into his skull.

"No, goddamnit!" His fist crashed onto the desk, sending pens and papers flying. "We won't be timid. Forget those idiots in Sycamore Canyon. We're accelerating our schedule and committing ourselves to our plan, all or nothing!" Beard wagging, voice rising, Greenfield raised his eyes to the ceiling. "We'll roast the towns of the West in flames and choke the people with smoke. Even if one or two people wander out of the wilderness with a few photos, they'll be buried in what we've done!"

"Yes! Yes!" Van Kamp squeaked. His fist pumped in the air and he precariously tottered atop his office chair.

Greenfield smiled. "Call the others." Then, suddenly, he was gone.

Van Kamp gazed in the direction of the departed environmental leader. The room was quiet, lacking the energy it had held just a moment before. A plate with a few crumbs and a crust of bread sat on the windowsill.

"Oh, shit."

Chapter 27

Jason's stomach rumbled again—a long, growling, whining eruption that seemed to evoke sympathy from above in the form of a simultaneous peal of thunder. He stopped in place amidst the long, boulder-strewn canyon floor, and clenched every muscle in his body in an effort to maintain control over his rebellious bowels.

To his right, Samantha also paused. Water dripped from her hair, which limply molded to her head and neck. She pressed her hand to her bare belly, grimaced, and met his eyes with her own.

Jason briefly lost himself in those eyes. He saw himself traveling through the woods with the owner of those eyes, exploring among the inner basin of the San Francisco peaks, grazing among the aspen ...

Another rumble interrupted his train of thought. He took a long suck of water to calm his stomach, gulping down the cooling liquid.

"I don't know," Samantha said. "The water tastes funny—worse even than the iodine. I wonder if there's something wrong with it."

Jason shook his head and forced a smile.

"I think that's just a little pond scum for flavoring. The iodine should take care of any critters."

"That's right," added Terry, who had joined Jason, Ray and Samantha in stocking up on water at Kelsey Spring. He wore his rain jacket, though it remained unzipped in front in a sort of solidarity-in-discomfort with his colleagues. "Besides," he added hopefully. "There hasn't been enough time for anything in the spring to affect us."

"So why do we all feel like shit?" grumbled Ray. He sucked at his water, started to spit it out, and then stopped and forcefully swallowed.

"Fuck. What's done is done. Right?"

Nobody spoke.

"Right," he answered his own question.

They continued in silence through the boulders, stretched out in a crude line from canyon wall to canyon wall. Free of stomach complaints, Rena and Bob walked ahead of the others. They gripped their rifles and eagerly looked for their prey.

Lightning flashed above. The searchers wound among the boulders and through the trees that lined the high ground near the canyon walls. Whoever the strangers had been, they weren't getting away if the dedicated staffers from the Center for Floral Supremacy had anything to say in the matter!

The floral supremacists' unhappy comrades were content to trudge in the rear, avoiding sudden jarring motions to the best of their abilities.

Jason stopped again. He hung his head and sighed.

"Guys, hang on a moment. I have to take care—"

A harsh, ripping noise interrupted his comments.

"What the fuck?"

Ahead, braced against a boulder, Rena held her rifle to her shoulder and squeezed off bursts of gunfire. Muzzle flash from the rifle lit up the canyon and the barrel bucked skyward as the animated fireplug poured bullet after bullet down the canyon.

Bob quickly joined Rena with a barrage of his own.

"Jesus Christ," Ray yelled. "Don't—"

Splinters of rock flew from boulders around them, and leaves clipped from trees parachuted to the ground. The duo's gunfire was being answered.

"Shit!" sounded from six throats and everybody dove for the nearest cover. Jason managed to land on his two-way radio and it squawked almost as loudly as he did from the impact. Then it stopped making any noise at all.

The rough landing pushed Jason over the edge. He clawed at the waistband of his shorts, pushing them to his ankles just in time. He spent the next several minutes grunting and cursing. With the gunfire at an end, a chorus of groans arose from the canyon floor and rebounded from the walls.

Finally, shorts back in place, Jason stood and brushed himself off. A thin trickle of blood ran where a sliver of rock had nicked him.

"Well, I certainly feel lighter."

He stepped forward, toward the spot where Rena and Bob cowered behind a flood-formed wall of earth and stone.

"What the fuck was that?"

"We saw them!"

"I figured that. I mean the *Apocalypse Now* scene. What was that?"

Bob shrugged.

"Well, that's what we usually do when we're shooting up car dealerships and the like. Except, nobody ever shot back before."

Rena stood.

"Sorry. But we didn't want them to get away."

"How much ammo do you have left?"

Rena's mouth opened slowly.

"Oh."

Samantha and Terry reappeared. Samantha looked a little flushed. She flashed him a smile, which he returned.

Terry shaded his eyes with his hand and peered into the distance.

"I don't see anybody now. Do you think you got them?"

Rena tilted her head and looked at the sky.

"Maybe not. I mean, I stopped shooting when the bullets came back."

Jason sighed. He looked around.

"Where's Ray. Damn it! Ray!"

Summoned, Ray stepped from his shelter among the rocks. All eyes immediately focused on him. He wore his shoes, daypack and sunglasses—and a shiny foil emergency blanket knotted around his middle.

"I wasn't fast enough, so I threw my shorts away. I don't want to hear a word about it."

He glared at them all. Then he took a sip of water.

Chapter 28

Scott dropped the empty magazine from his pistol without breaking stride, stuffing it into a pocket in his shorts. He replaced it with a full magazine, racked a round into the chamber, and then engaged the thumb safety before dropping the gun back into its holster.

"How many more of those do you have," Rollo asked. He gripped his .22 rifle by its plastic stock, waving it like a schoolroom pointer.

"Magazines?"

"Yeah."

"This is it. I wasn't expecting a gun battle with naked arsonists."

"Naked taxpayer-subsidized arsonists with the runs!"

Lani laughed.

"Hey honey. I'm glad you're not too freaked out." Scott hopped over rocks so he could comfortably put his arm around his girlfriend. Champ lent moral support, trotting along at the woman's side opposite Scott.

Lani folded her arms across her chest, and then lifted her face to smile at Scott.

"Oh, I'm freaked out. I'm completely fucking terrified. But I can still laugh when I imagine those maniacs suffering from a heavy dose of laxatives."

Scott and Rollo both laughed.

"Oh, I didn't have to imagine it," the older man said. "As we split, I saw one of them come out of the rocks wearing some kind of tinfoil instead of his pants. I'll bet he was out of action all through the fight." He shot a sharp look at the blonde woman. "Y'know. You may have saved our butts by dosing that water. Good thinking."

Lani jerked her head sharply toward Rollo.

"Thanks."

Scott cradled Lani's head in the crook of his left elbow, then kissed her gently on the bit of her forehead accessible below her rain hood. Then he peered up at the newly blue sky with its retreating line of storm clouds. He peeled back his own hood, and began wriggling out of his rain jacket without bothering to loosen his backpack straps.

"If you had big tits and lost that five-o-clock shadow, that routine would earn you big bucks in any strip joint," Rollo commented. He easily doffed his rain poncho, balled it up, and stuffed it back into a pocket in his pack.

"I can't do anything about the tits, but I'll try for a closer shave. I may need that money." Finally free of the jacket, which he crammed back into its stuff sack, Scott turned his attention back to Rollo.

"Speaking of ammunition, how much do you have for that pop-gun of yours?"

"Plenty. That's the nice thing about .22. It weighs so little that I always have a couple hundred rounds somewhere at the bottom of my pack."

"With all of those little bullets, you might give somebody a nasty bruise."

"Hey, I got them to keep their heads down."

The trio trudged along for a while, darting occasional glances over their shoulders. Champ again took the lead, scouting ahead and showing every sign of pure doggie joy in the extended hike. Despite the break in the rain, when possible, they stuck to the high ground by the canyon walls, avoiding the boulder-strewn stream bed where flash floods could catch the unwary. Blue sky overhead might be nature's own little game of bait-and-switch if a sudden squall at the head of the canyon sent a wall of water roaring down on them.

But trading low ground for high ground meant trading rocks for spiny plants that caught at their skin as much as at their clothing. Red scratches soon criss-crossed their arms and legs, transforming them into bloody tic-tac-toe boards.

Scott called a halt to the hike when the sky began to dim.

"We might as well make camp. We'll lose light pretty quickly down here."

Lani peered back the way they'd come.

"Do you think they're still behind us?

"Yep. Somewhere. But hiking this canyon in the dark is just begging for a broken ankle. They'll have to stop the same as us."

They settled on a small patch of relatively level, elevated ground. A ring of charred rocks marked where hikers had made camp in the past. Scott and Lani dropped their packs to the ground, and then quickly set up their shelter. They strung a line between two sycamore trees, then draped a lightweight tarp over the line and staked it out like an A-frame. A bug net was hung under the tarp, with a groundcloth to protect the campers from dirt and damp. They tucked their sleeping pads and bags under the shelter to keep them out of harm's way should the rain return.

Rollo sat on the edge of his blanket, which rested on a groundcloth, under the open sky. He sipped water, picked at his teeth with a twig, and cast an occasional gaze up the canyon.

"You folks have a shower in that set-up? How about a flush toilet?"

Scott moved a corner stake to tighten its attached line.

"It's only a tarp, Rollo."

"It takes long enough to get the damned thing up."

"It has head room for two, it keeps the scorpions out and it weighs less than that canvas beach blanket of yours."

The older man grumbled.

"I guess."

The sky flickered and a low rumble echoed from the canyon walls. An early star was visible directly overhead, but the canyon walls obscured any view of incoming weather.

Lani flicked on her headlamp, turning sycamore branches into shadowy, grasping arms reaching across the pale rocks.

"I'm hungry. Scott, I hope you brought the stove. And the food."

"Nope."

"No?"

"It's in your pack."

"Oh."

Lani disappeared under the tarp, the bug net draped across her elevated rump. She reappeared with a pot in one hand and a mesh bag full of cooking supplies in the other.

Scott took the pot from her hand and sat on the ground, using his folded sleeping pad as a seat. He lifted the lid and fished out a small metal cylinder, which he placed on an aluminum plate. A taller mesh cylinder wrapped around the metal cylinder.

Rollo rose from his blanket and squatted by Scott.

"And *you* call *me* MacGyver."

"It's just a stove. You've seen it before."

"You made it out of soda cans."

"Yep."

"Is that something they teach you on those fancy, East Coast trails?"

"Nah. Those trails are catered. I learned how to make this stove from the guy who introduced me to backpacking, many years ago."

"Your own, personal Yoda?"

"Sort of, if the little green guy was a danger to himself and others. That guy took me out during a winter thaw in New Hampshire. We were soaked and freezing even before he led us across a frozen creek—and then we fell through the ice. If he kept backpacking, I very much doubt that he's still alive. But he made a mean stove."

Scott removed a screw from a hole in the top of the central cylinder and squirted alcohol in from a squeeze bottle. He then drizzled fuel on the plate. Lighter in hand, he paused.

"Do you want to take a turn with the stove?"

"No thanks. I just think it's a cool long-way round to do something as simple as cooking a meal."

Rollo set to work gathering twigs while Scott placed the pot—now filled with water—over the hissing stove. He searched under logs and rocks for dry wood, which he dropped into his canvas hat. When the hat was full, he gathered several rocks as a combination wind-break and pot-stand, within which he quickly built a teepee of sticks and grass. Wisps of steam were already escaping from Scott's pot when Rollo touched a match to his construction.

"You sure you don't want to borrow the stove?"

"No thanks."

Rollo placed a small, soot-blackened pot over the fire and filled it with water. He threw in a handful of rice and another of dried vegetables, then began shaving pieces of jerky into the mixture. As he worked, he watched Scott pour boiling water into a thick plastic bag held by Lani. The water swirled around a dry mixture in the bag, which the woman sealed and put aside.

Rollo ostentatiously sniffed at his own concoction and gave it a stir with a battered metal spoon. He tasted it, added a dash of salt, and then tasted it again.

Lani picked up her bagged meal, jerked a hand away from the scalding-hot package, and then grabbed a bandana to use as a potholder. She gave the bag a squeeze, distributing the rapidly disappearing liquid throughout the saturated solid food. She unsealed a corner and sniffed at the escaping wisp of steam. She smiled approvingly, and then resealed the bag.

Rollo returned to stirring his pot.

"Oh for Christ's sake," Scott blurted. He produced a plastic spoon from the mesh bag and grabbed the meal from his girlfriend. He tossed the hot bag from hand to hand before dropping it to the ground, unsealing the zip-lock and plunging his spoon in.

"It's ready," he muttered around a mouthful of flesh-searing food. He then reached over and helped himself to a spoonful from Rollo's pot.

"Needs a few more minutes."

Refusing to meet Scott's eyes with her own, Lani clutched her own spoon and eagerly helped herself to dinner.

Rollo grumbled.

"What're you guys eating?"

"Chili," Lani answered. "I dry the veggies at home and Scott makes the jerky. We mix the dry ingredients together in the bag so we just have to add boiling water and let it sit for a few minutes to get a meal."

"Neat-o," Rollo muttered.

Scott snorted.

"I'm having beef stew," Rollo added, un-prompted. "I make my own jerky too."

"And very good jerky it is," Scott offered.

Rollo grumbled again.

"I wonder what the khaki-shirted bastards are eating."

Chapter 29

"Are you going to share that Power Bar?" Jason asked. "What for?" Ray snarled. "Eat your own food."

Jason glanced down at his bag of gorp—mixed raisins, nuts, M&Ms and the like—shrugged and took another mouthful. He chewed slowly, swallowed, and then surveyed his small band.

Terry sat on the ground with his knees under his chin and his arms wrapped around his shins. From time to time his right hand disappeared into his rain jacket pocket, emerging clutching a small, unidentifiable morsel which he guided to his lips. His eyes remained fixed forward, unfocused.

Bob, Rena and Samantha shared a large bag full of jerky. Samantha offered a chunk, which Jason gratefully accepted. He washed it down with a mouthful of water. The water tasted much better now that they'd dumped out their store and refilled the containers from puddles left by the rain.

"Thanks. It's good." He offered some gorp in return.

"Rena shot the cow herself."

Ray grunted, a sound that Jason ignored.

"Really?"

Rena nodded in satisfaction, sending a wobble through her goosebump-covered breasts.

"Yep. It was grazing on public land. It's good to make a political statement that tastes good, too."

Jason nodded, grimaced for a moment, and then finished his piece of jerky.

Samantha shivered slightly. The ground was damp from the day's rain and a light breeze stole the heat from their bodies.

"Are you cold?"

"A little chilled from the rain."

Jason pulled a light, metallic emergency blanket from his pack, identical to the one Ray now sported as a loincloth, and wrapped it around Samantha and himself.

Samantha smiled.

Ray scowled and Terry continued his thousand-mile stare.

"Guys. It looks like it's going to be a chilly night. Let's all gather 'round and share our warmth."

Bob and Rena eagerly moved to form a circle. Terry joined, slowly, when nudged.

Ray's scowl deepened.

"What's this group hug crap?"

"Don't you want to be warm?"

A rumble and flash announced the return of the rain. Around the group, dark blotches once again appeared on the rocks in a tightening pattern. The sky, which just a few minutes before had been speckled with early stars, now showed gray and featureless.

Ray's eyes bulged and his face reddened, but he moved forward to join his colleagues.

"Just don't fucking ask me to sing 'Kumbaya'."

Samantha snuggled closer to Jason, who sighed, softly, in contentment.

Chapter 30

The rain sounded a steady drumbeat on the tarp, beneath which Scott and Lani lounged, warm and dry in their sleeping bags.

Barely visible, just feet away in the gathering dark, Rollo sat cloaked in his blanket, with the edge of his groundcloth pulled up over his head like a cloak.

"I'd volunteer to stand guard duty," Rollo offered. "But somehow, I don't think it's necessary."

"Are you sure?" Lani asked.

"Nope. But I think any rangers stumbling around in the rain and the dark are more likely to need rescuing by us than to be a threat to us."

"Sounds like there's water flowing in the creek bed," Scott added. "It's a good night to drown in the desert."

They fell silent for a moment. The only sound was that of rain falling on rocks, brush and fabric.

Lani shifted positions, leaning her weight against Scott, who brushed his hand through her hair.

"Rollo, can I ask you something?"

"Sure. But I can't promise that I'll answer."

"You live out in the desert, and you don't work at anything steady that I know of. But when you come to town, you always have money for beer and hookers. How do you manage that?"

Scott laughed.

"Yeah, buddy. How do you manage that?"

The older man grumbled.

"Scott knows how I manage that."

"Oh yeah?" Lani turned her face upwards toward Scott's barely visible features. "How come you never told me?"

"It's Rollo's business, not mine."

"And a good business it is. Go ahead and tell her what I do."

Scott cleared his throat.

"This old bum is a big-time drug kingpin."

"What?"

"Oh crap, I'm fucking well not!"

"Well, you grow dope."

"What?"

"Yep. That part's true."

Lani sat straight up, brushing her head against the bug netting that draped down from the tarp.

"You've spent all these years out in the forest just so you can grow dope?"

An agitated rustling cut through the patter of rain.

"Oh hell no! I grow dope so I can buy supplies and have a little fun when I come to town. I've spent all these years in the forest to get the hell away from my wife."

Scott chuckled.

"That was Toni, right? I thought there was a little more to it than that."

"Well ... yeah. There was the house and the wife and the job. The house was one of those cookie-cutter deals in a quaint-by-decree town. Y'know, your fence can't be higher than five feet and you can't change your oil in the driveway and the neighbors come in three different flavors of pain-in-the-ass. It was perfect for Toni."

Lani leaned back against Scott, who nuzzled the top of her head and copped a feel—gently slapped away—under the cover of darkness.

"So, why'd you marry her?"

"She was a real looker when she was 24. There's no denying that. The sex was unbelievable."

"This seems to be something of a theme in your life."

"I know what I like. But when I married Toni I hadn't yet realized that a decent piece of ass could be had on a short-term rental basis; I didn't need to take on a long-term lease."

Scott successfully stifled a laugh, but Lani could feel the spasms through his touch and shot an elbow into his ribs.

"Jesus. I was just starting to like you."

"Can you tell he used to be a car salesman?" Scott asked.

"Bullshit. I sold insurance. What a racket.

"Anyway, Lani, if it makes you feel better, I didn't go over too well in that cookie cutter town either."

"Who'd ever guess?"

"Yeah. One of the town councilmen called me a 'menace'."

"Did you proposition his wife?"

"Nope. I just threatened to pour a load of concrete down his chimney. Him and his chums passed an ordinance banning new fireplaces. I just figured he ought to give up his own if he was gonna go and pass a law like that."

Lani reached back and stroked her boyfriend's cheek.

"Suddenly, I understand why you and Scott are friends."

"That's it," Scott joined in. "Rollo and I share a certain constructive disrespect for authority."

"No shit. But you're better than me at making up your own rules while making people think you're living by theirs. You blend in and subvert the system. I need to do things my own way, but there's not a lot of room left for that."

Scott hoisted his drinking tube aloft—a nearly invisible gesture in the dark.

"To Rollo, the last of the mountain men."

"So," Lani asked. "Did you do it?"

"What?"

"Pour concrete down the councilman's chimney?"

"Heh. I ain't telling."

A papery rustling interrupted the conversation. Scott thrust something into Lani's hand. She smelled the sweetness before she tasted the candy bar.

"Want some chocolate, buddy?"

"Sure."

Scott brushed the bug net aside. He launched the piece of candy into the darkness.

"Ow! Son of a bitch."

"Sorry. Your big head was the only thing I could see."

The night was filled with the sound of chewing. Eager molars crunched down on chocolate, peanuts and caramel.

"Damn that hit the spot."

"So," Lani began around a mouthful of partially chewed candy. She stopped, chewed some more, and then swallowed before beginning again.

"So, how'd you get from a life you hated to farming dope in the national forest?"

"Oh that. Well, my escape was always camping and hiking. Toni came with me at first. But she never much liked it and did it to make me happy. Later, she didn't much like me either, so I went off on my camping trips by myself to get away from things."

"Did you divorce her and decide that life in the woods was better than life in a model town?"

"Technically, I'm still on my last camping trip. It's going on six years now, so Toni and my boss have probably figured out that

I'm not coming back. Hang on ..."

The sound of a zipper cut through the night.

"Yep, here it is in my pack. I still have the airport parking receipt for my car. What a piece of shit. D'ya think it's still there?"

He chuckled and continued without waiting for an answer.

"Even buying nothing but occasional supplies, I ran out of cash pretty fast. And there wasn't anything left for an occasional blow-out in town. It wasn't long before I turned to a little part-time agriculture. Hell, it wasn't hard. That stuff will grow anywhere!

"Anyway, that's enough about me. What made you decide to torment kids for a living?"

In the distance a coyote howled, and was quickly joined by others of his kind. Silent until now, curled up at the feet of the sleeping bags, Champ responded with a low growl.

"I'll tell you—if you have a joint to share."

Chapter 31

The small circle clustered even more tightly as the coyote chorus continued. Jason snugged up against Samantha, Terry huddled between Bob and Rena, and Ray found himself pressed between the group's nominal leader and the mammal-hating fireplug. Damp and chilly under the thin, crinkly mylar of his now-tattered emergency blanket, which he'd spread out as a body-covering poncho, Ray inched away from his comrades. Almost immediately, he felt Rena's breast back in place against his arm. He shot a quick glance at her, and found his look returned by a sharp scowl.

"Can't we have a fire," Terry asked. Just a small one, maybe."

Jason briefly dragged his attention from the woman sitting next to him.

"Umm ... I don't think that's a good idea. Ray, you're the law-enforcement guy. What do you say?"

Ray sighed.

"It might just make us a target, and they're obviously armed and willing to fight. It wouldn't be a bad idea for one of us to stand guard, if anybody is willing to volunteer." He looked around the circle.

Everybody found someplace else to direct their eyes.

"Or not."

Ray glanced back at his neighbor and found her looking at him again. He felt a sudden flush of warmth—uncomfortable warmth. The coyotes chose that moment to raise the volume.

"Uh, I guess you guys don't like coyotes, right. I mean, they're mammals and all."

"Oh, that's not true. After all, they eat other mammals. I think that's pretty cool."

"Yeah," Bob added. He hunched forward to meet Ray's eyes, barely visible in the gloom. "It's really a misconception to say that we hate *all* mammals. We just can't stand the destruction that some mammals wreak upon the wonderful, defenseless world of plant life. But carnivores are fine; we have nothing against coyotes."

Jason cleared his throat.

"I think coyotes are pretty cool, but they have nothing on deer. Deer are so sensuous." He paused. "Is it sensuous or sensual, I always get those confused?"

Ray's jaw fell open.

"Deer?" Samantha asked. "But they're herbivores! You can't like plant-eaters."

"I think it's 'sensual'," Terry added.

"No, really," Jason objected. "They have those firm, muscular flanks, and those glistening, moist eyes—"

Oh wow, Ray thought.

"Oh wow," Samantha said. "That's exactly how I feel about manzanita. I love how the warm red color of life flows through the stalks during the Monsoon. The bark is so smooth and—"

"Oh yeah." Bob said. "Manzanita are way ... sensual? Is the word 'sensual'?

"Prickly pear, too. The contrast between the bright red fruit and the thrusting thorns is just ..." his voice trailed off.

"Erotic?" Rena asked.

"Yeah. Erotic."

Terry stirred, the hood of his rain jacket bobbing in the dark.

"Oh man, that's so cool. I've never felt that way about anything."

"Anything?" Jason asked.

"How about people?" Ray asked.

A long silence ensued.

Ray sniffed. His head shot up. He sniffed again.

"What the hell? Is that marijuana?" He stood and inhaled deeply. "Goddamnit. That's illegal! I can't believe that we're chasing those scumbags, and they're having a pot party."

Ray suddenly felt chilled once again. Cool air moved over bare skin—lots of bare skin. He looked down. His silvery emergency blanket clutched, uselessly, at his ankles. Rena stared at him—at least, at a point on him about half way up. Her eyes didn't waver.

Flushed and confused, Ray grabbed the thin mylar sheet and draped it around himself like a toga.

"On second thought, I think I'll go stand guard duty."

Chapter 32

Scott awoke with the sun. The first pale splashes of light were hazily visible on the canyon's walls through the thin green tarp, though the sun had yet to visit the floor of the canyon. Between these high rock walls, a clear view of the sun itself was hours away, and Scott hoped to be on the trail long before he stood in direct sunlight.

His bladder felt heavy and close to bursting. A quick glance revealed Champ sprawled across the tarp's two human occupants, with his head on Lani and his hindquarters resting on Scott's midsection. The dog snored softly and one paw twitched in accord with some fragment of canine dream.

Scott eased himself out from under Champ and slid from his sleeping bag. The dog stirred and raised his head in response to the commotion.

"Stay."

Champ whined, yawned widely, and then flopped back down on his mistress's belly.

Lani shifted in her sleeping bag, and then was still again.

Scott's bladder still felt heavy, even free of the dog's weight. He quietly eased his feet into his hiking shoes, tucked his pistol into his right hip pocket, raised the edge of the bug net, and ducked out under the sky.

The ground was damp underfoot, as if it had rained again in the early morning hours. Confirmation for that theory was found in the cigar-like configuration of Rollo's bedding, which he had rolled around him as protection against the weather. Only the top of the older man's head and the tip of his nose were visible. Loud snores issued from these projecting features, easily drowning out Champ's efforts.

Scott walked into the rocks up-canyon from camp and found a likely spot in which to relieve himself. The early morning chill felt bracing, like a quick cup of coffee, but he was more than happy to tuck everything back where it belonged when he was finished.

He started back toward camp, and then stopped and glanced further up-canyon.

"Hmmm."

A few minutes later, he slipped from rock to rock, listening for tell-tale sounds, though he wasn't quite sure what they might be. In shadow among the rocks as he was, he wasn't too worried about spying eyes. Still, he stepped carefully to avoid setting small rocks rolling and sending up a clatter that might alert his pursuers.

Despite the cool air, he started to sweat. A bead of nervous perspiration rolled down his face. As much as he wanted to know what the fire-bug rangers were up to, he didn't want to be caught sneaking up on people who had unloaded impressive quantities of ammunition at him just a few hours earlier.

That ammunition might have come from official sources, but he suspected the rangers wouldn't follow official procedures if it came to an arrest.

He froze as a low noise eased its way across the canyon floor. It repeated. It sounded almost like a chorus of low, warning growls—like something a pack of wild dogs might emit if a stranger wandered too near the den. He followed his ears, carefully, to a raised clearing along the canyon wall.

Up close, the noise became clearer and less threatening. It was snoring—a *lot* of snoring. He peeked around a large boulder.

"Holy shit," he hissed.

In the clearing, huddled together on the ground, lay the firebugs. They were wrapped in sparse coverings including emergency blankets, a rain jacket and uniform bottoms. Chests rising and falling almost in unison, they clearly shared a moment of contented deep sleep.

Day packs and rifles were arranged in a tight circle around the tangle of human bodies. Scott briefly considered approaching closer to gather up the rifles. He put his hand on the butt of his pistol as he considered the idea. Then he thought of his odds against the bunch if they awoke while he was festooned with more weapons than he could handle. He withdrew, slowly and quietly.

Back in camp, the tarp was already down and packed away, and Lani had the stove going. Rollo sat on his pack, gnawing a piece of jerky. Champ sat attentively next to him, closely eyeing the dried meat.

"Hey, honey. I'll have some coffee ready in a minute," Lani said. "Where were you?"

"I scouted out the folks who are chasing us. I'm not completely convinced they're Forest Service."

"What?" Rollo spat a piece of jerky to the ground. "Who in hell do you think was shooting machine guns at us?"

"Rollo, they're all sleeping half-naked in a pile."

The older man's eyes widened.

"They had an orgy?" Lani asked. She laughed.

"No, they're only *half* naked. I think they're trying to stay warm. Aside from the guns, they have almost no gear. Considering what I just saw, and that weird ceremony we interrupted yesterday, I'm favoring the idea that we've run up against some bizarre cult."

Rollo spat again.

"What about their trucks and uniforms?"

"They only have pants. Hell, maybe they *ate* the real rangers and used their shirts for napkins. If that's the case, that would suggest they're marines. But that seems improbable."

Lani stood with a steaming metal cup in her hand, which she handed to Scott. He took the cup and elaborately kissed her hand.

"So we're being chased through Sycamore Canyon by a pyro death cult? How likely is that?"

Rollo grumbled in obvious agreement.

Scott sipped his coffee and sighed.

"Well … it's a lot more likely than the idea that we stumbled on a band of naked homicidal rangers holding a torch-lit forest-burning ceremony."

Chapter 33

Fingers clenched in a white-knuckle grip on the steering wheel, Ranger Tim guided a government-issue SUV of not terribly recent vintage at wildly excessive speeds down Interstate 17. With the gas pedal pinned to the floor, Tim kept his badge visible on the passenger seat next to him. He felt the comforting weight of his Sig pistol on his hip.

In his present mood, Tim wasn't sure if he'd resort to the badge or the gun if pulled over by a Department of Public Safety officer. He hoped the green truck with its official seal would discourage a traffic stop, but it was no guarantee. He wasn't in the mood to be interrupted—his mission was far too important for that—so he kept his options open.

His own Park Service supervisors had provided the truck; the Forest Service, in the person of Martin Van Kamp, insisted that it was running low on available vehicles. Van Kamp rubbed in the point that Tim himself had been responsible for one of the trucks lost in the fire down Woody Mountain Road. Tim smarted at the memory of the conversation. It was one more reason for him to rush to his destination and punish the people who he saw as the cause of his humiliation.

Nobody accompanied Tim. He'd been clear on that point.

"I don't want you down there alone," Van Kamp whispered in a gentle, soothing tone. "You should have backup. We already know these people are dangerous."

"I don't want anybody along to get in the way," Tim answered.

The Chief Ranger waved his hands dismissively from behind his desk. Even propped up in his chair as he was, the effect was a bit like a kid reaching to pull himself over a wall.

"Nobody will be in your way. They'll be there to help. You'll be in charge."

"Help?" Tim rested his hands on the desk and leaned forward—and downward—to face Van Kamp. "Help like Jason 'helped'? Help like the tree huggers 'helped'? If I get more help like that all I'll need from you is a few kind words at my funeral."

Van Kamp managed a weak smile as he pushed back from his desk. His chair thudded into the file cabinet behind him and his arms wagged wildly as the chair tilted, and then righted itself.

"Uhh ... no. No, I can get you better people than that. I'm sorry—"

Tim shook his head.

"I don't care who you get. I don't want 'em." His lips skinned back from his teeth in a feral grin. "Damnit, Van Kamp. I don't want any *witnesses*."

Hours later, speeding past the Stoneman Lake exit and down the highway as it descended steeply from the high country, Tim exulted in the focus and freedom he felt in his solitary mission.

As the packed-dirt emergency pull-off ramp came into view, the acrid smell of overworked brakes filled the air. He didn't worry a bit; the problem couldn't be with his truck. He hadn't touched his brakes since he'd started the engine.

Chapter 34

Rollo took the lead as the trio of renegades tramped their dusty, sun-drenched way down-canyon toward … well, they didn't really know what they tramped toward, but they were all too aware of what lay behind them.

"My cache is somewhere up ahead."

"Where?"

The older man pointed up and to the right. Scott followed the line of his finger to the canyon wall. The rocks rose sheer and steep, broken by ledges and sharp projections of stone. Here and there a shrub-like tree clung for dear life to a few square feet of gravity-defying soil.

"Up there."

"On the canyon wall?" Lani asked. She shielded her eyes with a hand and craned her head to spot where the two men were looking.

"Christ no. Up on top. On the mesa, but further down the canyon. I'm not sure how far." He paused for a moment, and then shielded his own eyes. "That does look kind of high, doesn't it?"

Scott stood in place and contemplated the towering canyon walls. Sycamore Canyon wasn't the deepest gouge in the Earth that Arizona had to offer, but that was a long way up—and back down.

"You climbed up that with your gear?"

"Well … no. I came in over the trail from further up the the canyon."

"Screw that." Scott said. He started walking. "I don't think this is the week to learn how to fly. We'll head straight for the canyon mouth."

Lani nodded her head vigorously and mouthed her silent agreement. Scott smiled and put his arm around her. He leaned over and kissed her on the lips.

"Why don't you and Rollo walk ahead. I'm going to keep an eye on our back trail just in case our naked friends are after us again."

Lani nodded.

"Half-naked."

"What?"

"Our half-naked friends."

"Yep. Them."

Lani called for Champ who was clearly torn over who to accompany. He looked at Scott, then at his mistress, and whined. Finally, he padded over to Lani grinning and panting. Dog in tow, she stepped forward and fell in alongside Rollo.

"Wanna fool around?" Rollo asked after a few paces.

"*What?*"

"Oh hell. I thought I'd just get all that awkward sexual tension out of the way.

"Jesus Christ. You are the biggest—"

"Asshole. Yeah, I know. I've learned to live with my limitations. It's a curse, y'know. Sorta like hemorrhoids."

They walked in silence for several long minutes. Champ dashed ahead, scrambling over rocks and perching atop boulders for views of the trail down the canyon.

The sun was nearly overhead now, and temperatures rose to

match the glare and the dropping elevation. Lani stripped down to a T-shirt over her shorts, while Rollo grudgingly pulled off a tattered windbreaker, leaving his trademark plaid shirt in place.

Lani suddenly giggled.

Rollo snorted.

"All right, I'm sorry."

"That's OK. You were trying to get a rise out of me, and you did it."

Rollo smiled.

"Yeah. I did."

"Dick."

"Sorry."

"So, you think we're going to get out of here."

Rollo grunted. He said nothing for a long moment, then answered.

"Fuck. I hope so. I like Sycamore Canyon, and I don't especially mind dying here. But I don't want to be shot by a bunch of psycho rangers who are trying to set me up as a firebug."

"You still think they're rangers? Scott said they slept in a pile, with no sleeping bags and too little clothes. And that scene yesterday was just as weird."

Rollo sighed.

"OK, that's strange. But they had Woody Mountain Road sealed off. That sounds pretty official to me. And then there's the business with my cabin. That truck I … umm … liberated was Forest Service. I don't think a bunch of nutjobs with a pack of matches are behind this."

"Maybe." Lani sounded doubtful. "Anyway, I think Scott's plan for getting that video out is a good idea."

Rollo grunted.

Lani shot a glance at her traveling companion.

"You don't agree?"

"Scott has more faith in people than me. I'm not convinced that video is going to help us. Even if we get it to some journalists, they'll probably spin it as hardworking civil servants doing their jobs. We'll end up the bad guys."

"You think Scott has faith in people? He doesn't even like them! Look at the way he lives his life. I mean, I love him and all, but he does his own thing, in his own way. He's not exactly a stickler for obeying the law."

Rollo stabbed a sharp look at the woman.

"You have it all wrong, Lani. Scott likes people just fine. It's groups he can't stand, and the control freaks that try to run groups. People get tribal when they're in groups and start slapping around anybody who doesn't conform. Scott gets along all right with individuals." He looked back down the canyon. "I sort of agree with him. But I still think he cuts people too much slack."

"You are a natural-born hermit."

"Damn straight. And I look forward to getting back to hermitting."

Lani laughed again. "Well, maybe you're right. He's nice enough to my students when he meets them."

Rollo glanced out of the corner of his eye.

"Is it true you let your kids screw-off in the forest instead of going to class?"

"Is that what Scott told you? I can't believe— No! I let my students have more leeway than I'm supposed to, and I get them interested in lessons by letting them do things they enjoy—"

"Whoah. Hold on there."

"No, I'm pissed. I take my job seriously—"

Seeing Rollo laughing so hard that tears streamed from his eyes, Lani stopped.

"You got me again."

"Yeah. Scott approves of what you do with the kids. So do I, by the way. Not that you need my approval."

"I just get so much shit for doing things a little differently."

"I don't doubt it. The schools aren't set up to teach kids. They're just supposed to keep the little punks docile and get them used to obeying orders."

Lani sighed and took a long sip of water. She kicked at a rock and watched Champ go scurrying after it.

"Is this another Forest Service conspiracy?"

Rollo looked thoughtful for a moment.

"Nah. Probably not them."

"Rollo, the people I work for aren't competent enough to plot the corruption of young minds. They're just time-servers who like to do things by the book so nobody gives them any trouble. And they hate giving kids more freedom or being questioned because that suggests that they're not experts who should be calling all the shots."

The man scratched at his face and sniffed.

"Maybe so. It's all the same in the end."

Lani nodded.

"Yeah. It is."

Back from his pursuit of the wandering pebble and pressing in from the side, Champ leaned up against Lani's left leg, causing her to stumble. She caught herself before toppling over face first, but as she stepped forward again, the dog stepped back in her path.

"Damnit Champ. Are you herding me?"

The woman gave in and moved in the direction suggested by the animal. Then her thoughts froze in response to a sound like a solo performance by the world's most enthusiastic maraca player. In the grip of adrenaline and instinct, Lani, Rollo and Champ lurched away from the noise, covering about ten feet in the blink of an eye.

Rollo kicked a small rock toward the sound's source—a coiled reptile poised for a quick strike.

"Shit! Rattler."

Out of reach of the snake, Lani hunched down and stroked her dog's face.

"Wow, Champ. Thanks."

Rollo eyed the animal thoughtfully.

"That is one good dog."

Chapter 35

At a safe distance from reptilian threats, but all too close to two-legged dangers, Scott hiked along in the shadows by the canyon's wall. The route was treacherous with rocks and tangled with thorns, so he moved slowly.

He also kept an eye on the trail behind him. The divided attention made him move even *more* slowly, and he began to regret his impulsive decision to play rearguard. He'd intended to be stealthy, hanging in the shadows to see how much of a lead he and his friends had over the pursuers—and to slow them down if he could. Now he feared that he'd end up playing tag in a rocky corridor with a pack of homicidal maniacs.

Seeking reassurance, Scott reached for his holster. His thumb easily slipped into place, disengaging the snap that held the restraining strap and allowing the pistol grip to fill his hand. He brought the pistol up, simultaneously disengaging the thumb safety.

Now he felt armed *and* nervous, which was infinitely better than just being nervous.

Sound carried far, but unpredictably, between the walls of the canyon, and he heard his pursuers long before he saw them.

"I'm still stiff from being so fucking cold last night."

"Rupert says that discomfort is an artifact of Western

materialism. We're too used to luxuries."

"Who the fuck is Rupert?"

"So people in Massachusetts don't get cold?"

"Western means our whole civilization, not just the American West. You know, America, Europe, Australia ..."

"I repeat—who the fuck is Rupert?"

"That's Dr. Greenfield."

"So people in Tibet don't get cold?"

"I'd like to see Dr. Greenfield spend a night in the open under a piece of tin foil."

"Oh, he does. Rupert denies himself most pleasures. He thinks we all should so that we're less of a burden on the Earth."

"Especially on the plants."

"Of course. Especially on the plants."

"All pleasures? Like what?"

"Oh sure. The people of the developing world know how to live with nature. What we consider discomfort they see as a normal way of life. It's very spiritual and in tune with the natural rhythm of life."

"Well, like heat and air conditioning and new clothes. He's worn the same clothes for years. He doesn't wash them, because that consumes resources."

"Christ. Why doesn't he just suck off a shotgun and *really* reduce the burden ..."

"I'm having a hard time believing that people in Tibet don't get cold."

Listening in the shadows, Scott slowly shook his head. "I can't believe I'm running from these people."

He peered down the canyon. In the distance, people came into view, gesturing wildly at each other. Their movements were slightly out of sync with the echoes from the canyon walls, but sound and vision made it clear that the animated discussion had degenerated into an argument.

"How can you say that about–?"

"Rupert sounds like a fucking loon! That's all I'm—"

"There's no fucking way they don't get cold—"

Scott raised his pistol.

"I'll be doing them a favor, honest to God. At least, I'll be doing *me* a favor."

Scott sighted in on the largest of the pursuing rangers. He focused on the pistol's front sight, the target's crew cut blurring into obscurity as his finger squeezed the trigger...

Shit! He couldn't do it. Dangerous lunatics they might be, but he wasn't yet at the point where he could just shoot one down in cold blood.

Feeling like an ass, Scott changed the point of his aim to a rock just in front of his original target. The man walked along, punching the air with his hand, lips moving seemingly without connection to the sound rebounding from the canyon walls.

"Well, if he's such a fucking genius—"

"All I'm saying is that cold is *cold*—"

"He's a sensitive, brilliant lover of plant life–"

Lover of plant life? Scott wondered. Literally? What in Hell is that all about? What are they? Psycho grad students? That might narrow it down to Forest Service, after all, or NOAA—those fish-and-wind types are pretty freaky. Or a few other agencies, to be honest. But the pyromania and armed pursuit ... He pondered on his questions as he squeezed the trigger.

An explosion rolled through the canyon, smothering the sounds of argument. The lead man staggered and dropped like a sack of cement, leaving Scott wondering if a ricochet had made up for his squeamishness. The man's comrades disappeared almost as quickly, though a foot or a rump poked out here and there from inexpertly taken cover.

"Hold it right there you tree fuckers!" He was still fixated on the last words to echo through the canyon before his shot. "I've had it with this shit. Throw out your—"

Scott never got to finish his command. A burst of automatic gunfire sounded, followed by the insect whine of ricochets and the crashing of branches falling to the ground. He ducked behind a boulder and covered his head with his hands. At a lull in the firing he peered out and squeezed off a shot at a faint glimpse of motion. Then he dropped to his hands and knees and began crawling as quickly as possible back up the canyon toward Rollo and Lani. A quick look behind him revealed a head rising from behind a distant bush. He fired again. Then he continued his scurrying way among the sharp rocks and sharper thorns, his gun hand cocked at an angle to keep the pistol out of the dirt.

Ten long minutes later he stopped to assess his various nicks, cuts and bruises. A long scratch down his right calf oozed red. He doffed his cap to scratch his sweaty scalp and noticed a neat bite out of the brim where a bullet had apparently passed.

He fingered the damaged fabric while thinking back on his moment of restraint just before firing his warning shot. He punched himself in the thigh.

"Dumbass."

Chapter 36

"I thought we discussed the whole shooting frenzy issue yesterday," Jason said to his assembled team. He fumed and glared at his comrades, who gathered behind as much cover as they could find in the wake of the ambush.

In return, the targets of the ranger's wrath kicked at dirt, sniffed and nervously eyed their toes. That is except for Ray and Samantha. Ray glared right back, while mopping with the back of his hand at a red pattern of dots that might have been freckles if they weren't oozing blood down his cheeks. A spray of rock fragments sent flying by a bullet had left their mark on his face—and his mood. The combination of the bloody freckles with the shiny, though somewhat tattered loincloth had Jason thinking of a cartoon character ... Baby New Year! That's it. A really belligerent Baby New Year recovering from a bender.

In contrast, Samantha just stared back looking wide-eyed and slightly hurt. Jason battled to keep from sinking into those damp orbs. Well, and the firm, if dusty orbs below. They weren't large, but he just wanted to sink his face between—

He caught himself.

"Well, didn't we?"

Bob cleared his throat.

"Uh, sorry Jason. That was us." He indicated himself, Rena and Samantha.

Rena waved.

Samantha shrugged and eased out a rueful smile.

"What happened?"

Bob started to speak, and then hesitated.

"Really. I want to know why you've shot off most of our ammo."

"Well, that *is* how we're used to shooting."

"Yeah. We talked about that."

"And then there's that whole 'tree fucker' thing. That's just wrong, and I think we're a little sensitive."

Ray refocused his glare on Bob. His mouth opened to speak, but froze in place. His lips tightened and he shook his head. He emitted a deep sigh.

Terry stared off into space, squinting and obviously lost in thought. His eyes suddenly widened.

Jason was intrigued though not very surprised, but decided to stick to the issue at hand.

"Well, did you at least hit anything?"

"Oh sure!"

"Really! Let's go see if he's—"

"Oh. You mean the guy shooting at us. No, I'm pretty sure we missed him."

Chapter 37

Lani was nervously pacing around a small clearing with Champ dogging her heels when Scott caught up with his friends.

"Told ya," Rollo said to the woman. He sat under a stubby tree with his pack at his side and his rifle across his knees. An uncapped water bottle sat within easy reach.

"You look comfy," Scott said. It was all he could get out before a blonde cyclone flew across the clearing and buried herself in his arms. He returned her attention for a long moment, every bit as happy to see Lani as she was to see him.

"Well, one of us had to get comfortable. She's been wearing grooves in the dirt. But I told her you'd come back all right."

"You had faith in my abilities?" Scott had reclaimed his lips and now buried his face in Lani's hair. "Shucks."

"Some. More than that, though, I figured that a gunfight is a heroic way to die. You're not the type to go out all that heroically. You're more a die-in-a-compromising-situation kind of guy."

"Thanks."

Reunited with his girlfriend, Scott spared a moment to rub Champ's head, acknowledging the affection of the beast who stood almost erect on his hind legs, leaning against the couple and licking both their faces.

"We heard the gunshots," Lani said.

"Yeah. I got stupid and fired a warning shot. They responded with World War 3."

Rollo snorted, snatched the hat from his own head and threw it against the ground, doing the aged fabric no perceptible harm. A cloud of dust rose around the brim, and then settled in place. The hat's fabric blended in as if camouflaged.

"Now are you convinced they're trying to kill us?"

"Yeah. I am."

"What do they want?" Lani asked.

"I'd guess they're not happy that we witnessed whatever it was we saw in the forest, but I don't know. You need to see them. It's like being chased by a well-armed circus sideshow."

"You teach them any manners back there?" Rollo asked.

"I taught them to keep their heads down; but they did the same for me. I don't think they've given up, if that's what you mean." He paused. "And that brings up a point. The firebugs outnumber us, are better armed than we are and apparently have a shitload of ammunition. We've been lucky so far, but they could easily catch up with us."

Rollo grunted. Lani crinkled her forehead—a smudge of dirt clung there, left by her clinch with Scott—and glanced nervously down the canyon.

"Then, shouldn't we get mov—"

"*You* should get moving. You and Champ with the phone and the video."

He handed over a folded piece of paper.

"Here's the log-on information for the mailing-list server and my YouTube account. Just find a cell-phone signal, upload the video and send the information as an e-mail formatted like it says."

"*What?* You have to be kidding me! I'm not going anywhere without—"

"He's right," Rollo said.

"No he's fucking not!"

Rollo sighed and shuffled his feet.

Scott jumped in.

"If Rollo and I stay back and block the canyon, you have a much better chance at getting through with that footage we shot of the forest fire being set. Then we can get some help."

It won't do us any good if they come up behind us when we're unprepared." His voice softened. "And honestly, honey, we can't always watch our backs."

Lani nodded.

Scott reached out with his phone in his hand.

"Here's the video evidence. Remember to upload the file before sending the email. You OK with that?"

Lani hesitated, staring at a spot on Scott's chest. Champ picked up on the mood. He looked at Scott, then at Lani, and whined. Simultaneously, the two humans patted his head.

Lani chuckled. "You're a good doggy daddy."

"Yeah, well. He resembles your family more. That schnozz of his …"

Lani hit him.

Rollo cleared his throat.

"I think you should get going. There may not *be* any more bad guys by the time you get that video delivered."

"You're going to get them all with that .22?"

Rollo shook his head.

"Hell no. I got me a jen-you-wine battle rifle in that cache. With plenty of feed to keep it happy."

Lani looked straight up.

"Way up there?"

"Well … yeah."

Scott raised his eyes, visually scaling the nearby cliff, and gazed at the rim above. Crags, ledges, sharp ridges of rock and tough, gravity-defying vegetation rose to meet the sky. He shuddered.

Rollo chuckled.

Scott tore his eyes from the view above and began pulling at the velcro straps holding his pistol holster in place.

"What are you doing?" Lani asked.

"Giving you my gun. You remember how to use it, right?"

"Uh … yeah … why?"

Scott gave a last tug and freed the strap from his backpack's hipbelt. He handed the pistol over to Lani, whose mouth hung slightly open as she accepted the gift.

"Remember, use your thumb to disengage—"

"Yeah, I know. Why?"

"Just in case they sent someone to the trailhead. I don't want you walking into trouble. You have three … no, *four* rounds in the magazine."

Lani stared at the gun, and then began weaving the strap through the loops on her own hipbelt. When it was finally fastened in place, the slab of Colt-manufactured steel wore her more than she wore it, but Scott grinned his satisfaction.

"Do I look all right?"

"You look dangerous, baby."

"Are you all set?"

Lani nodded.

"I am if everything is on that paper."

"I wrote it all down just in case. Go on ahead, baby."

"Here?"

Scott glanced at Rollo, who looked back up at the cliff. Rollo shrugged.

"We might as well climb here."

Scott took Lani's hands.

"Yep. Here."

Lani's lip quivered.

"Don't get yourself hurt."

"Oh Christ," Rollo muttered.

"Shut up," Scott said. "No, not you." He squeezed Lani's hands.

"Be careful."

"You be careful too. Whoever these people are, they're mean as snakes"

A few feet distant, Rollo snorted.

"Snakes ain't so—"

"Shut up," Scott and Lani said in unison.

Rollo muttered.

Scott and Lani kissed, long and deep. Forcing himself to break the clinch, Scott pulled himself away. He dropped his pack to the ground and transferred some gear between his pack and Lani's pack. Then he bent and rubbed Champ's fur.

"You watch out for her buddy."

Lani looked back over her shoulder as she walked away. She grinned and tugged at the fabric of her shirt.

"I'll have clean clothing before you!"

Scott waved.

"Don't worry, baby. When we meet back up, you won't need any clothing at all."

Rollo looked after the departing woman and shook his head.

"I wish you hadn't said that."

"Why?"

"That got me all worked up. And now I want a hooker."

Chapter 38

Some distance up the canyon—further than Scott and company had any right to hope—Jason was also all worked up. Obscene as his thoughts were, though, they didn't involve hookers.

"You fuckheads are *not* turning back!" His face bulged red and a vein throbbed in his temple. "We didn't come this far to run away just because those bastards shot back at us!"

Unaccustomed to overt displays of anger—or, indeed, of any strong emotion—Jason aped the mannerisms of Chief Ranger Van Kamp to express his outrage at his wavering crew.

Terry, Jason's fellow ranger, recognized the familiar mannerisms. But even he didn't realize that his colleague's uncanny impression of their tiny boss was less an expression of rage than of gut-wrenching fear. Jason shook not with anger, but in terror of what Van Kamp and his co-conspirators would do to the bearer of bad news if the team returned empty-handed.

"Hey, calm down," Terry suggested. He backed off a judicious few paces. "We're just saying that this all seems a little more serious than we anticipated."

Bob nodded.

"I think that guy was actually trying to kill us."

Jason glared.

"Were you or were you not trying to kill him? That's why we're here, right?"

"Wait," Terry said. "We're actually trying to kill them?"

Five pairs of eyes bored into the ranger. The moment stretched out in silence. A shadow flickered across the group from the passage of a hawk overhead. Terry glanced up at the bird, which was starkly outlined against a patch of blue sky. He winced as Ray slapped him in the back of the head.

Bob shrugged.

"Well, yeah. I'm just not used to people shooting back."

"They do that sometimes."

"I guess. Are you sure we shouldn't turn back? Who would blame—"

Ray growled. It was an animal noise that started low in his chest and erupted from his throat. His scraped, dirt-streaked body and metallic loincloth underlined the savagery in the sound.

"Nobody turns back." He gripped his rifle so the muzzle pointed at the ground between Bob and Terry. "I'll be damned if I'm walking out of the forest looking like this without something to show for my trouble."

"That's the spirit," Jason said. Appalled as he was by Ray's implied threat, he was thankful that somebody else shared his desire to go forward—and was willing to prod the others along. Still, he had the strong feeling that he had somehow become a passenger on the out-of-control rollercoaster of his own life. He shook it off. "Get your gear together. We're heading out."

Lifting his depressingly light daypack, Jason felt someone brush up against him. He turned.

"Hi," Samantha whispered. She pulled a strap from his pack over his shoulder and eased it into place. "You were so forceful, just now."

"Oh, I—"

"I really liked it." She met his eyes. "Really."

A few yards away, Ray snorted and turned in disgust. He ran smack into Rena. She looked up at him with a smirk on her face.

"You don't look so bad to me." She tugged at a tattered strand of his emergency blanket. "Really."

Ray shuddered.

Chapter 39

$\mathint{S}$cott reached for a handhold to pull himself to the ledge above and winced as a sharp pain stabbed through his finger.

"Son of a bitch."

He retrieved his hand and stared dolefully at the long thorn embedded in the last joint of his right index finger. A sharp yank removed the thorn, but it left behind a burning sensation out of proportion with the small wound and tiny drop of blood.

"Watch out for cactus," Rollo called from below. "They're a bitch."

"Thanks."

Scott carefully chose another handhold and hauled himself to the ledge above. He cursed as his knee scraped across a rocky outcrop, drawing blood. Once safely atop the ledge, he kicked dirt fitfully at the prickly pear lurking just behind the edge, where he'd first placed his hand, but took care to avoid entangling his foot in the plant's spines.

"Gimme a hand," Rollo called.

Scott knelt and stretched out his arm. Rollo caught hold and scrambled as the younger man pulled. They sprawled together on the ledge, which was wider than it seemed from below.

"You think we're half way up?" Rollo gasped.

Scott glanced up at the sky where a line of storm clouds

threatened yet another Monsoon soaking. His eyes traveled to the rim, still far above.

"No. We're maybe a third of the way up. If it makes you feel any better, it looks easier from here on. You almost have a stair case for the next 50 feet or so."

Rollo sat up for a look, and then promptly lay back down.

"Yeah. All we need are eight-foot legs to match and we're all set."

Scott wiped sweat from his face. His skin felt warm with sunburn. He had sunscreen in his pack but, as usual, he'd forgotten to grease up. He doffed his pack and set to rectifying that error now. While he smeared himself with white cream, he stared up the canyon, looking for movement.

"I don't see anything behind us yet."

Rollo propped himself up again to see for himself. He brought his hand to the brim of his hat, providing his eyes with a little extra shade.

"Nope. Nothing."

"We'll have to hustle if we're going to get to the top and dig up that rifle of yours before the bad guys get passed us."

Rollo sighed and looked straight up at the long distance yet to be climbed.

"Or ..."

"Yeah? I'm open to alternatives."

"Why don't you tell me where you stashed your stuff. I'll climb up and get it while you keep watch for the bad guys."

The older man looked hopeful for a moment, and then slumped.

"It's a good idea, but there's no way I can tell you how to find the cache. It's not like I can draw you a map."

Scott slapped his forehead.

"Don't you remember where you buried your stuff?"

"Mostly."

"Mostly? What the hell does that mean?"

Rollo sighed.

"Well, it's been a long time. And I hiked in to make the cache; I didn't climb a cliff. When I get to the top, I'll have to look around and orient myself before I can even start looking."

"Shit."

"Well ... yeah."

"So we'll go up together."

Rollo was silent for a long moment. Then he cleared his throat.

"What happens if those bastards pass us while we're up on top?"

Scott looked down the canyon the way Lani and Champ had gone. He thought he saw movement that might have been them, but it might as easily have been an animal or his eyes playing tricks. He didn't speak.

"I'll have to go up alone," Rollo added.

"And I'll stay here with the .22."

"Yup." Rollo sighed again. "Oh shit." He slid his arms from the straps on his pack and rose to his feet. His arms stretched out before him, fingers laced together, palms facing outward. The knuckles cracked together with a noise like the breaking of a handful of dry sticks.

"Wish me luck."

"If you bring back something more powerful than this popgun, I'll give you more than good wishes."

Rollo squinted and cocked his head.

"I don't swing that—"

"Cold beer, you asshole."

Rollo smiled.

"You do love me after all. In a traditionally masculine way, that is."

"Get going."

Rollo set off, levering himself onto the first giant stair leading to the rim above. He made good time, and soon his figure dwindled in the distance, like a bug crawling up a wall.

Chapter 40

Rollo didn't much mind making the climb alone; he'd lived alone by choice for years, after all. He wasn't happy about splitting the tight little group three ways, though. As much of a loner as he was, he firmly believed that safety lay in numbers—though safety in well-armed numbers was better yet, and he had to admit that his .22 rifle and dwindling supply of ammunition wouldn't keep them whole and happy forever.

Besides, Scott had been his close buddy ever since that half-remembered encounter by the Flagstaff police car (Rollo had been drinking his way through town at the time, so he'd needed the details filled in after the fact).

"We did what?"

"We slashed the tires on a cop car. Don't you remember? It was only half an hour ago."

"Well ... that's embarrassing. We didn't get caught, did we?"

"No. No, we didn't get caught. Are you sure you want another beer?"

He worried about Scott. His friend didn't need to be in this situation and wouldn't be at risk if Rollo hadn't dragged him into his long-running feud with the Forest Service.

As for Lani ... the self-styled mountain man hated to admit

it, but he enjoyed sparring with the little blonde firecracker. He didn't exactly *like* her, but she kept him on his toes—and she wasn't hard to look at either.

Hopping from one rocky ledge to the next, Rollo bounded like a mountain goat on native terrain. Harried as he was, he still felt a bit of his usual exhilaration at being out-of-doors and beyond the reach of civilization with its rules and expectations. The air tasted cleaner, his mind seemed clearer, and he felt like dropping his shorts and wagging his sunburned—yes, sunburned—ass at the whole world of rangers, ex-wives, cops and debt collectors.

In fact, he had dropped his pants to the world on many occasions; some of them by the light of a (he assumed) sympathetic moon shining above. But there had never before been an audience to appreciate his sentiments, and he didn't have time to take advantage of the audience he had at hand.

As his efforts took him close to the top, he slowed, briefly, to admire a cluster of stud-like projections from a slab of stone. He'd seen their like in the area before.

"Fossils. Cool."

As Rollo knew from experience, the southwestern landscape, with its petrified forests and deep-cut canyons slicing through layers of rock, is like an unlabeled museum of Earth's ancient history. You might never know for sure what you were looking at, but you could be certain there was a hell of a story behind it. Once again, he reminded himself to take the time someday to try to identify the long-dead things that had catalogued themselves here into the museum of nature's permanent exhibit.

If he ever made it to town again, that is. He decided not to dwell on that point.

The top of the rim came up sooner than Rollo had any right to hope. He was drenched with sweat and bleeding from scratches on the palms of his hands when he pulled himself up on a final ledge, and then shimmied through a narrow gap that had him sucking in his gut.

He looked around. The mesa top was dominated by juniper trees and well marked with cow pies left by local ranchers' cattle.

"Excellent," he muttered. "Now, where the fuck did I bury that stuff?"

Chapter 41

With the men behind her, essentially guarding her back, Lani felt more secure than she had since the whole misbegotten adventure had started. The safer she felt, the more guilt nibbled at her conscience over feeling secure when Scott and ... well ... yeah, Rollo, too ... were staying behind to face the lunatics dogging their tails.

Within a few hundred yards, Lani had herself worked into a tearful frenzy. She would have turned back if she could figure out a way to get Champ to climb the canyon wall. But she couldn't. So onward she went.

Attuned to his owner's moods, Champ whined and licked Lani's hand. When she paused to look back the way she'd come, he pawed at her for attention. She ruffled the fur between his ears reassuringly. He rubbed his muzzle against her leg in response, leaving a small drool stain on the fabric of her shorts.

Despite her doubts, she started walking again. She resigned herself to setting one foot in front of the other for as long as necessary. There was no point to what the men were doing if she didn't get the video to somebody who could help.

What form that help would take was anybody's guess, and the uncertainty set Lani to fretting again. She removed Scott's instructions from her pocket and glanced at the carefully printed text. She was no computer whiz, but her boyfriend knew that and had rendered the instructions as detailed as he could, and in plain English. It still looked like nonsense—a bit like asking somebody for driving directions and getting a monotone recitation of *Jabberwocky* in response.

"Why couldn't it have been literature, damn it? Or correcting papers? I'd feel a lot more comfortable if Scott had asked me to stop the firebugs by marking up some essays in red pen."

Champ gazed up at her sympathetically.

"Well," she added. "I'm also good at playing the guitar. Why couldn't he have asked me to help out with some blues chords? There *are* things I'm good at, just not computers."

She wasn't sure, but she thought Champ nodded in agreement.

"Thanks, boy. I'm glad you're with me."

The dog grinned back, and then lifted a leg to piss on a prickly pear.

The sun shone overhead, with no clouds visible in the slice of sky revealed between the canyon walls. The sway of Lani's pack and the rhythmic slosh from her water bladder set a cadence as she hiked along. It was easier to concentrate on the hike than on what lay behind or ahead, so she kept her mind on the trail and did her best to take pleasure in the scenery.

Enjoyment came more easily than she'd anticipated. With Scott and Rollo laying for the firebugs, she no longer felt a need to look over her shoulder. She was finally able to appreciate the simple fact of being outdoors. Exploring the desert was one of her favorite activities, and she soaked up the details: the rapidly evaporating pools of water left by the rain, the flitting lizards evading her steps, the scrubby trees and brush. Refreshed by the monsoon rains, the vegetation showed an unusually vivid green that emphasized the natural beauty of the normally dry area. With an experienced eye she dodged sharp desert holly that lured with pretty leaves and tore at unsuspecting hikers' skin.

Twice she passed by small cairns left by earlier hikers. Each marked a faint trail that wound up and into the distance. Tempted though she was, she knew that any diversion from the canyon floor itself would leave her truly on her own; Scott and Rollo would have no idea where she was. Worse, Rollo had warned his companions that, while trails official, unofficial and recognized solely by the animal kingdom did wander through the area, the best she could hope for was to emerge on a jeep road miles from help—or even water. Other trails just led further into wilderness.

So onward she walked.

It was several hours later, as the shadows grew longer, when she heard gunshots behind her, in the distance.

Chapter 42

With Ray leading the way, Jason's team trudged slowly, tentatively and with varying degrees of enthusiasm (or lack thereof) down the canyon. As if to make up for the recent rains, the sun blazed down and glared off the rocks and in their eyes. The blue sky overhead featured a few puffy, postcard-ready clouds that carried too little moisture to so much as settle the rising dust.

Monsoon season was like that—drowning you one moment and baking you the next.

The group had made remarkably little progress in the past few hours—nobody but the silver-diapered park ranger seemed enthusiastic about rushing ahead. Terry and Bob, in particular, favored frequent rest stops and a slow pace.

But they all realized that only a severe case of sunburn camouflaged the red flush of Ray's rage. Nobody revived the earlier conversation about turning back.

"Take it easy, Ray," Jason cautioned. He did his best to inject confidence into his voice so he'd sound like he was in charge.

"Why?"

"So you don't get yourself ambushed."

The man responded with a growl.

"If I go any slower, we'll be going backwards."

"Well … be careful."

Ray snorted.

"If you're worried about me, let somebody else take point."

"Uh … sure. How about—"

Ray whirled around.

"I know. How about Bob?" He cupped his free hand to his mouth. "Hey, Bob, you courageous cow killer. Get your ass up here!"

A faint voice drifted from the end of the column.

"Ummm … What do you need me for?"

"To take the lead. Jason wants you to test for traps and such."

Jason's eyes widened.

"Hey, that's not what I—"

"Get up here, Bob!"

The dejected-looking activist stepped slowly to the front, his rifle dragging from his hand. The skin of his chest and shoulders was filmed with sweat and dirt. His wispy beard was caked with a rime of salt from dried perspiration.

"Jason, I don't know that I want to do this."

Jason placed his hand on the environmentalist's shoulder in what he hoped was a reassuring gesture.

"It's all right. We'll all take turns."

Ray chuckled.

"No worries. Bob's a seasoned combat veteran. He'll do just fine." He stepped closer to Bob. "If anybody shoots at you, just think of him as a mammalian menace."

Bob seemed to slump in his skin.

"OK."

The column got underway once again.

"Don't worry, Bob. I'm sure—"

The unhappy activist's rifle flew forward, out of his hand, as he fell backward. Red spurted from his shoulder.

Newly developed reflexes sent the rest of the team diving for cover before they were consciously aware of the gunshots echoing from the canyon walls.

Chapter 43

Scott heard the bickering long before he spotted any targets. "Oh, Jesus Christ," he muttered. "Not again."

He glanced up the face of the cliff, looking for a sign that his friend was returning. He got a double eyeful of nothing for his trouble. The rocks and shrubs hung as still as photographs, revealing no motion.

The rains of the previous day were a forgotten memory, and each breath was molten.

"Shit."

His face was wet with perspiration, which oozed past the sweatband of his cap. Individual drops of sweat crawled across his scalp with a sensation like tiny bugs marching in column. Pulled low over his eyes, what remained of the bullet-damaged brim of the cap cut the glare and gave him a clear view of the canyon floor.

Reflected by the high walls of dirt and stone, disembodied voices tramped through the canyon like an expedition of dyspeptic phantoms—perhaps the ghosts of ill-tempered cowboys past.

Though Scott would have liked to believe that real-life cowboys wouldn't sound so much like a married couple counting the days to a nasty divorce.

Lagging behind the flapping of lips, a lone figure came into view around a bend in the canyon. A moment later, his—or her—companions followed.

Remembering how his earlier mercy had been repaid, Scott didn't hesitate to bring his borrowed .22 rifle to bear on the leader. Sprawled prone on his rock ledge, he rested the barrel on his balled-up left fist. He peered through the peep-hole rear sight, focusing on the front sight resting against the blurry image of his target, and slowly squeezed the trigger.

Accustomed to the kick of his .45 pistol, he barely noticed the slight recoil of the little rifle.

He'd fired four rounds before the first answering shots etched the stone around him.

Chapter 44

The seatbelt held Tim in place as the Park Service truck lost its traction through the curve on the dirt road and slipped sideways. Break, gas, steering wheel. He operated the controls simultaneously, in a combination that would have been catastrophic if catastrophe weren't already under way.

He had time to contemplate the on-coming ditch and brace himself before the world turned upside down. The engine screamed, Tim screamed and the truck shuddered through a roll. Over, over, thump! His head slammed into the thin padding of the roof. Something crunched and the windshield shattered before his eyes.

Instinctively, he clamped his eyelids shut.

The truck came to rest. Tim hung suspended sideways by his seatbelt. He fumbled with the clasp and unfastened his restraints, immediately tumbling into the passenger seat. Now he was wedged in place. The cab of the vehicle confined him, the air clouded with dust drifting through the new gap in the windshield.

Tim struggled to right himself, caught between the seat and the dashboard. Losing skin in the process, he forced himself into a more traditional orientation with gravity: feet down, head up. At least, he thought that's how it was—he couldn't really see through the choking cloud kicked up by the accident.

He found the driver's-side door handle and pushed. The door, miraculously, opened, then fell back down into place. He pulled himself up, pushed again, and climbed out of the cab of the truck.

Moments later, he stood above the vehicle, by the side of Sycamore Canyon Road, assessing the situation.

Tim felt bruised and battered, but not injured in any important way. A sizable knot was forming on his head, but that seemed to be the worst of the damage.

The truck looked worse, but not mortally injured. The front windshield was shattered and dents marred nearly the entire surface of the vehicle. The engine had stopped sometime during the roll, which caused Tim some concern, though he was vaguely thankful that the crash hadn't turned into a fiery wreck. He remembered plenty of movies in which crashes automatically turned into balls of flame. He didn't know how close Hollywood crashes came to the real deal, but he figured a temporarily dead engine was better than premature cremation.

The most serious issue seemed to be the truck's orientation, resting on its side at the edge of the ditch like a sick beast. However intact its vital parts might be, the truck wasn't going anywhere until its tires once again touched earth.

As Tim examined the mess, his relief at coming through the wreck unscathed began to morph into rage at betrayal by his means of transportation. His face grew red and he charged back to the truck. He braced himself by the roof and leaned his full strength and weight against the wounded vehicle. It rolled forward, and then rocked back. He pushed again. It rolled again, a little farther, and then rocked back against him, threatening to topple over and crush him beneath its weight.

Unheeding, Tim threw himself against the vehicle once more. It moved, teetered on the edge of either a final return to its wheels or a crashing flop onto its back. He called on reserves of strength and pushed just a bit more.

The truck slammed into the ditch, rocking on its suspension with its wheels once again in contact with the ground. All was right—at least right*er*—with the world.

The moisture in his body seemed to have migrated from his mouth to his armpits, where it rapidly evaporated through the fabric of his shirt into the Arizona air. Wheezing a little, Tim fetched his backpack from the truck's enclosed cargo area and sucked a long draught through the water hose. He checked his hip—his gun was still in its holster.

An inspection tour of the truck revealed a new problem: the right rear tire was blown. He didn't have a chance of getting back on the road, let alone to the trailhead, until it was fixed.

Soon, sitting on the spare tire with a lug wrench in his hands, he wrestled to remove stubborn lugnuts. One nut didn't want to budge; whoever had last put it into place had paid no attention to the threads. Instead, they'd just cranked at it until it refused to turn any more. He put his full body into turning the wrench, leaning with his weight until it creaked and, suddenly, gave way.

A sharp pain shot through one finger. Howling, Tim peered at the mangled tip. The nail was torn almost completely away. Blood oozed and then dripped from the finger and down his hand. He whimpered slightly, then stood and hammered his uninjured hand on the roof of the truck.

He caught his breath and forced himself to sit back down. He removed the remnants of the nail, and then went back to work.

The spare tire went into place in short order.

Tim left the jack and the ruined tire lying in the dirt as he made his way to the driver's door and eased himself into the seat. A trail of red drops marked his passage. He rested the lug wrench on the dash and slipped the key into the ignition. It turned.

Nothing happened.

He turned the key again.

Not a whisper or a groan came from the engine.

With an animal growl, Tim erupted from the truck. He slammed the lug wrench into the hood, leaving a deep dent. He backed up and cocked his right leg, unleashing a powerful kick into the left front quarter panel.

Something stretched and snapped in his ankle. He dropped to the ground with his mouth open in a silent howl. With his eyes screwed closed, bright flashes of light synchronized with the throbs of pain. He couldn't quite catch his breath.

He had no idea how long he'd been there when he heard the engine noise. It was a low buzz, off in the distance, but growing louder.

Dragging the injured foot, Tim climbed up the edge of the ditch and back onto the road. Every step was an agony.

There, down the road, he could see a vehicle approaching. It came closer, closer. The distinctive outlines of a Subaru Outback emerged through shimmers sent up by the desert heat.

Favoring his right ankle, the battered ranger limped to the middle of the road. He waved for the car to stop. The lug wrench wagged from its firm grip in his left hand, dried blood crusted his right arm, and a large knot distorted the outline of his head.

"Slow the fuck down, goddamnit," Tim screamed. He waved his arms frantically.

The car seemed to slow momentarily, then put on a burst of speed. With a roar it rushed past him.

Tim coughed and spat dust in the wake of the speeding Subaru. It skidded into a turn and disappeared around the bend, chased by his curses.

Sweating and filthy, the enraged ranger threw his lug wrench to the ground. It landed ineffectively in the dirt. He limped over to the wrench, picked it up, and hurled it again. This time, it bounced off the hard-packed dirt of the road, flew across the ditch, and smashed into the driver's-side window. The safety glass shattered into hundreds of round-edged fragments.

Red-faced, Tim clenched his fists and screamed. Then, he sagged and sighed. Laboriously, he eased himself down into the ditch and retrieved his backpack.

Moments later, he began hobbling, ever so slowly, along the long road leading to the Sycamore Canyon trailhead.

Chapter 45

Truth to tell, one patch of scrubby forest could look pretty much like another patch, even to a seasoned desert rat like Rollo. Fortunately, Rollo was experienced enough to know that, and he had a hatful of tricks for marking trails and recording the location of caches. He knew to take sightings on prominent and permanent—well, permanent in human terms—landmarks. He left cairns and other signs that he could read, but that didn't reveal too much to outsiders.

Then again, time and imperfect memory have a way of defeating even careful planners, let alone cheerful misfits with a taste for beer and fine dope.

"Goddamnit!" Rollo yelled for the third time in ten minutes.

Dirt caked his arms up to his elbows, as well as his knees and chest. A base layer of grime etched by streams of perspiration marked his face like aboriginal war paint. Before him a two-foot deep pit gaped dark and empty. Within easy view, two other holes of equally recent vintage bared their emptiness to the sky, promising nothing but sprained limbs to unwary travelers.

"It's around here. I know it."

The sun burned blazed in the sky, heating his hat until it felt like a campfire smoldered over his pate. He spat dust, and wished he'd been smart enough to bring a water bottle when he'd dumped his pack. This was supposed to be a quick trip up and back—that's what he'd promised Scott, anyway. Instead, it had turned into a scavenger hunt. And he was the scavenger, burrowing into the earth with his hands and a broken branch for want of anything better.

He was sure—almost sure—that he had the right place. The scenery looked familiar. He'd found what he knew was an old blaze he'd carved in a tree, and then, a few minutes later, another.

But that scattering of rocks ... Was that what the years had done to one of his old cairns? Of the others, he'd seen no sign. Animals walking by and seasons of rain could easily have tumbled the stones in all directions.

That left him digging at random in the general area of his old cache. He hoped. And so he burrowed into the ground with his hands, tossing a plume of dirt in the air behind him like an inept badger and challenging the durability of his increasingly creaky knees.

Crap.

Something chattered mockingly from within a thorny pile of scrub a few yards ahead of him.

"Chee-chee-chee-chee."

He wrapped the fingers of his right hand around a clod of earth, damp from the recent rain, and compacted it into a ball. He flung the missile as hard as he could.

"Laugh at that you fuc—"

Overbalanced by the pitch, he lost his grip on the edge of the pit and slipped forward into the hole. His hands shot out to grasp the edges but slid through the crumbly earth without gaining any traction. A moment later, he spat soil from between his lips and sent up another round of curses to singe the sensitivities of the wildlife.

As he pulled himself out of the pit, his fingers brushed against something hard and curved. He quickly dug into the wall of he hole he'd made, revealing a piece of what was clearly a large, plastic cylinder.

"Hallelujah!"

Some time later, a five-foot length of PVC pipe capped at both ends lay on a pile of loose dirt (and one of Rollo's fingernails). Sweaty, dirty, bleeding from a half-dozen minor abrasions, and looking more feral than ever, Rollo laughed maniacally.

The feral man gripped one of the caps and began to twist. He grunted. He sweated some more. Finally, he stopped to catch his breath. He examined the cap closely.

"Son of a bitch."

Now Rollo lay down, clamping the cylinder between his knees. He gripped the cap with both hands and exerted himself again. A wild grin played across his face.

Slowly, the cap began to turn.

Chapter 46

"**W**hy am I the only one shooting back?" Jason screamed. He crouched behind cover that consisted of a manzanita bush and a few rocks—not much protection, but all he had at hand. His rifle poked through the bush, resting loosely on a branch. He crouched as low as possible, grasping the rifle with just his right hand and squeezing off rounds with little attention paid to aim.

"I'm shooting," Ray answered calmly. He knelt behind even sparser cover, firing aimed shots at a spot well up the canyon wall. A twig near his head exploded into fragments, and the man barely flinched before firing again.

Jason glanced around, looking for somebody or something else to focus on other than the person trying to kill him and his colleagues.

"What about the rest of you?"

Terry sat well to the rear, leaning against a bank of earth carved by the high water brought by Monsoon rains and spring snowmelt. He covered his head with his hands and rocked back and forth.

"Shit," Jason muttered. He looked to Samantha and his eyes softened. She smiled back.

"Is there anything—?"

She held up a magazine from her rifle and pointed it toward him so he could see that it was empty.

"Oh shit."

She pointed to where Rena carefully tended Bob's wound out of sight of the shooter ahead.

"Them, too, I think." She shrugged sheepishly. "Sorry."

Jason began sucking wind in convulsive sips and the world seemed to spin. He let go of his rifle and cupped his head in his hands. This expedition was supposed to be an idealistic lark. He and his comrades had set out to drive human habitation from the high desert pine forest in the name of all that was good and green.

That was his dream, after all. He wanted to wander through a world devoid of people—except for Samantha, of course. He was pretty sure she was on the same wavelength, which made this whole project even more worthwhile. To find somebody who cared about the same things that he did, and who wanted to depopulate the world so they could share it alone—well, together, but otherwise alone—was exhilarating.

Yeah, things got a little dark when they were spotted and started chasing the strangers. But it was fun to be the one doing the chasing. And those strangers wanted to stop him from completing his mission—or at least they had the potential to do so.

But now he was the one in the crosshairs, and he didn't like it one bit. His whole fantasy about the Carthage Option was beginning to take on a new meaning. Instead of imagining himself as a Roman conqueror, sowing the defeated lands of Carthage with salt to keep them from being inhabited again, he saw his role transforming before his eyes. Maybe he wasn't on the side of the Romans in his Carthage Option; maybe he was that guy who rode the elephants ... Hannibal! That's right. Hannibal was the Carthaginian general.

Did he really ride elephants?

Never mind.

Anyway, Hannibal had started out as the invader, chasing and defeating the Roman troops, but he ended up losing everything. That would suck. He didn't want to end up as Hannibal, watching everything he believed in get destroyed.

"What?"

Jason was jerked back to reality. He looked around and spotted Samantha looking at him. She leaned forward, almost beyond the limits of her cover.

"Huh?"

Samantha brushed her face with the empty magazine from her rifle and spoke again.

"Did you just say you don't want to ride an elephant?"

Chapter 47

Rollo's eyes teared a little, and his mouth felt like he was sucking on a ball of cotton. Blinking away what felt like bits of gravel from his eyeballs, he descended carefully down the cliff face on his way to the ledge where Scott, to judge by the gunshots, had introduced himself, once again, to the firebugs.

"Damn this shit," he cursed, blinking again. "Tastes like I'm smoking a mummy's cock."

The mountain man paused, braced himself with one hand on a crumbly chunk of sandstone and used his free hand to pull the ancient joint from between his lips. He grimaced and shook his head. He tried spitting, but nothing left his mouth other than a short burst of bad breath.

He sighed, returned the joint to its perch at the left corner of his mouth, and continued his journey.

Climbing down was more difficult than climbing up for several reasons. One reason was that the descent required him to actually look where his body would fall if he lost his grip on the rocks and shrubs that provided his natural ladder. Then there was the battering his rear was getting from the rifle slung over his shoulder. As promised, he'd retrieved the cached battle rifle and hung the heavy piece of wood and steel on his back by its canvas sling. He already had awkward bruises on his back and thighs to show for his efforts. Accompanying the rifle was its ammunition, which bulged from his pockets and from a bandolier slung across his chest. As he climbed, the cartridge boxes wore through the well-aged fabric of his clothes, dug into tender spots and left bruises to match those left by the rifle.

And then there was the joint. He hadn't even remembered caching dope with the rest of his supplies, but there it was: a full freezer bag begging to be rescued from its subterranean repository. He'd stuffed it down his shirt, except for enough to fill a rolling paper.

The stuff really hadn't aged very well at all. It was also throwing off his balance and his depth perception.

"Fuck."

He rubbed at a nasty scrape on his calf.

A final drop brought him to … well, that wasn't very final at all. There was still a last scramble to be made across an area that would expose him to fire from below.

Rollo thought about the situation, and then almost immediately decided that reflection was a bad idea. Allowing himself as little time as possible to consider the danger, he clenched his teeth around the joint and lunged.

"Oh shit!"

"Rollo! I'm— Oh my God. Did you set fire to your underwear?"

The would-be hermit spit the last of his joint into space and pressed his gut into the dirt. The belly flop drove his stuffed pockets into his flesh and he felt sharp lumps digging into places that ought to, as a matter of policy, remain unmolested by hard metal projectiles.

The impact drove the wind out of him, so he couldn't respond immediately.

"I'm serious. What's that stink?"

"An excellent vintage of northern Arizona loco weed."

Scott tilted his head to stare at the source of the bad odor.

"You had that in your cache? Why?"

Rollo wriggled the rifle sling from his shoulder and pushed the rifle forward. The wood and dark steel slid through the dirt until the muzzle projected beyond the ledge and the trigger was by his hand. He lifted the bolt handle and drew the bolt back.

"I don't really know why. I'm sure it made sense at the time. It still does the job, anyway."

"Still does the job? Then leave that stuff alone right now."

Rollo bristled.

"Hey, I spit it out. OK?"

A light tattoo of gunfire from below chewed the rocks and dirt around them—far around them. Somebody wasn't taking the time or effort to aim.

Rollo finished transferring ten tarnished brass cylinders, tapered at the front, from his right breast pocket to the rifle's magazine. He pushed the bolt forward and then locked the handle down.

Scott fired a few rounds from the .22 to keep the firebugs' heads down, then turned his attention to the older man.

"A hunting rifle? I thought you said you had some kind of assault rifle up there."

"A battle rifle," Rollo answered. "This is an Enfield. The Brits used it during World War II."

Scott eyed the weapon dubiously.

"I don't doubt it. Does the museum curator know his exhibit is missing?"

Rollo sniffed and flipped the rifle's rear sight so it stood straight up. He ostentatiously fiddled with the adjustments, dialing the peephole up and down to find the proper range. Then he realized that the adjustments were all for ranges far beyond the actual distance of their enemies, and dropped the sight back down in favor of the larger, non-adjustable sight.

"I suppose I should be thankful you didn't fetch back a crossbow," Scott said.

"Shut up. You'll see."

Rollo ostentatiously took aim through the rear peepsight. A bush behind which he'd seen some movement blurrily filled the ring of the rear sight, overlayed by the blade of the front sight. He carefully put pressure on the trigger. More … more …

Both men jumped. Then they peered over the edge of the ledge. Aside from the ringing in their ears, the canyon was silent. There were no shots from below, no animal noises, and no birdsongs to challenge the memory of the rifle's bark.

"Well," Scott said. "That makes a wonderfully loud noise, but I don't think you actually hit anything."

Chapter 48

Particles of exploded juniper tree floated in the air, catching stray rays of sunlight and lightly sparkling. They were beautiful, but Ranger Jason Hewitt found the aesthetics of the moment clouded by the fact that the beauty had been produced by a small chunk of metal traveling at supersonic speed.

"What the fuck was that?" Jason shouted.

"A gun," Bob answered in a low groan.

"A big gun," Terry mumbled, barely audibly. He'd abandoned his seated rocking for a position face down in the dirt, and his words were muffled by a mouthful of soil.

"I know that. What happened to that little popgun and the pistol they were using before?"

"Well fuck," Ray said. "I don't know. Maybe they traded up." Despite his bravado, he crab-walked to better cover at Jason's immediate left. The move challenged the little modesty permitted him by his foil loincloth, and he rested his rifle against a rock to tug the thin plastic back into position.

"Why does it matter?"

Jason turned and stared.

"Don't you think it's a problem if the people we're chasing can go shopping for new weapons when they're perched on a cliff in the middle of the desert?"

Ray grumbled.

Another explosive "crack!" split the air. There was no visible impact, but a whine like a giant hornet passing overhead indicated a ricochet up the canyon.

A movement to the side caught Jason's eye. He happily turned from Ray and fears about armories in the wilderness to stare into Samantha's wide eyes. Her face was pale—where it wasn't caked with dust.

"Well, at least whoever is shooting isn't getting near us," she chirped, considerably louder than necessary.

Ray lunged to close the distance with the woman. He barked from all fours.

"Shut up! They don't need any help!"

Chapter 49

"Somebody down there agrees with me," Scott said. Peering through a low bush, he surveyed the canyon below. "You're a lousy shot. Either that, or that museum piece of yours is no good."

Rollo spat.

"I don't see you knocking those bastards over like bowling pins."

"I nailed their point man before you even got back here."

Rollo lifted his head from the stock. He looked thoughtful.

"You did?"

"Yep."

"Shit. I'm sorry I missed that."

He slid the heavy rifle across the dirt to Scott and reached for the .22.

"Trade you."

"You want me to try my hand?"

"Why not? Sounds like you're our resident sniper."

Scott hefted the rifle. It was as heavy as it appeared. The metalwork, including the receiver, bolt handle, magazine and muzzle were all a dull black color. The wood was dark brown and non-reflective. It looked lethal.

The bolt action was similar to that of the few hunting rifles he'd handled, but there was no scope mounted on top. Still, the sight was easy enough to figure out. You peered at the front sight located near the muzzle through a wide ring mounted on the receiver—a similar setup to the sights on the little .22 rifle he'd been using. If you lined up the sights properly, the bullet went, more or less, where you looked.

"Go ahead," Rollo urged. "Let's see you do your stuff."

Scott lifted the bolt handle and drew it to the rear. An empty casing shot from the chamber, arcing back and to the right. It made a cheery ringing noise as it clattered against rock. He pushed the bolt forward to pick up a round and insert it into the chamber. The bolt resisted being returned to its position, and then gave up the fight as he slid the handle back into place.

He rested his cheek against the stock of the rifle. The world became what he could see through the ring and beyond the front sight: brush, trees and rocks. Vague movement fluttered past his tunnel-like field of vision. He scanned the rifle slowly, right to left, across the canyon. A flash of light on something metallic caught his eye. He focused. Air slipped out through his lips. His lungs reinflated half way, and then he stopped his breath and took up the pressure on the trigger.

The gun leaped. Something banged into his forehead.

"Ow. Son of a bitch!"

"Oh yeah. Watch that. That rifle has quite a kick."

"Thanks for the warning. What's that howling sound?"

Rollo peered into the canyon. He hooded his hands over his eyes and stared at a flurry of activity on the ground below.

"I'd say you're a better shot than me after all."

"I told you so."

Scott pressed himself forward and joined his friend in a dangerously exposed position, leaning out into space for a view of the damage he had wrought.

In the air, carried on the slight breeze, a small fragment of silvery foil-like material fluttered and scattered the sunlight.

Chapter 50

A high-pitched scream split the air. It echoed and rebounded from the canyon walls, which seemed to magnify and refocus the aural assault on the small party scurrying among the rocks.

Jason gritted his teeth as he slowly dragged Ray's writhing body around the bend in the canyon to—if only temporary—safety. The wannabe-G-man weighed more than the expedition leader, so Jason's mission of mercy proceeded at a snail's pace until Samantha jumped in to lend her muscles to the effort.

"Oh Christ," Ray moaned. "Would somebody please shut him up?"

Jason and Samantha turned to stare at Rena, who stopped in mid-stride on her way to offer help. She in turn glanced back at Bob, who clutched at his bandaged shoulder. Bob shrugged—a lop-sided motion that caused him to wince. He walked over to where Terry lay curled in a fetal position on the ground and kicked the man, sharply, in the ribs.

The screaming stopped.

Terry shot bolt upright, snuffled and wiped at his eyes.

"You didn't have to do that."

Bob tilted his head and gave another half-shrug. He walked away.

Under a razor-leafed desert holly, Jason and Samantha deposited their cargo. He instantly yelped in pain.

"Take it easy, man," Jason mumbled as he bent to check on Ray's wound."

"Take it easy yourself. It feels like I'm on fire."

Rena muscled Jason aside, almost sending him sprawling. She kneeled by the patient and poured water from their dwindling stock over the wound.

Looking over her shoulder, Jason involuntarily sucked air through his teeth.

"What?" Ray demanded.

"They shot your ass off."

"Funny! Really, what—"

"I'm serious. Your ass has a divot in it you wouldn't believe."

"It's OK," Rena cooed, her breasts swaying pendulously. She patted gently at the injured man.

"I'll patch you up. You'll be just fine."

Ray sighed.

"Thank God somebody here has some medical training."

Rena paused, and then leaned to one side so she could meet Ray's gaze.

"Oh, you mean that nasty Western stuff? No, I use traditional healing techniques."

Jason braced himself for a tirade from the man on the ground, but instead of yelling he just seemed to droop.

"Please tell me ... please ... that traditional healing includes something that resembles an antibiotic."

The kneeling woman pulled bandages and a vial of something from her pack. She began to chant.

"Huh," Bob said. "She didn't chant for me." He looked at Jason. "This must be serious."

Jason forced himself to smile. He gestured Bob away from their makeshift hospital bush and called for Samantha and Terry to join them.

Terry snuffled a bit. Jason shot a concerned glance at his colleague, but said nothing.

In a huddle, his arms around Samantha on one side and Terry on the other, Jason forced himself to act more cheerful than he felt.

"Well ... Things haven't gone exactly as we planned. We're a little low on ammo and supplies. We have two injured team members. And the enemy seems to ... well ... be better equipped than we'd anticipated."

Samantha met his eyes with her own soft, wide orbs. Once again, he felt himself falling into their bottomless depths.

Bob's reedy, strained voice snapped him back to reality.

"Yeah. And I don't think Ray is as gung ho now as he was a few hours ago."

Jason nodded.

"That's probably true. I think we need to reappraise the situation."

"*Reappraise?*" Terry shrieked. "I can give you my appraisal. "We're fucked."

Chapter 51

"Where are all these damn hippies coming from?" Martin Van Kamp wondered aloud.

He stood outside the Beaver Street Brewery, south of the railroad tracks that ran through Flagstaff. A train rumbled by just a block away. It was early evening—too early for one of the two passenger trains that still rolled through town, serving the dwindling number of travelers who cared to pay more money for less-convenient service than they could get from the bus companies. That meant a long freight train was inching its way from one side of the old lumber-and-rail town to the other, helping the residents slow their pace of life—whether or not they appreciated the assistance—by cutting the town in half during its journey.

Van Kamp belched. He decided his Mongolian beef salad and hefeweizen tasted just as good the second time around. The scent of smoke hanging in the air from the now officially dubbed Woody Mountain fire actually enhanced the flavor.

"I mean," he added. "I know this is a college town, but this is starting to look like that scene from the Hitchcock flick ... you know the one I mean ... "

Failing the test in film history, his companion, the BLM official, remained silent and stony faced.

"*The Birds*! That's it. Except this time with damn hippies."

The two men surveyed the picnic tables along the edge of the parking lot, and the sidewalk in front of the coffee shop across the street. Sure enough, they were more crowded than usual with t-shirted, clove-smoking, bike-riding twenty-somethings who, apparently, had some time to kill.

Van Kamp was troubled. It wasn't that patchouli oil and sandals were all that new to the area. To the contrary, they were a regular part of the scenery. Flagstaff wasn't just a college town, it was a college town in the mountains with easy access to ski slopes, climbable cliffs, hiking and biking trails and ATM machines. These characteristics exercised a powerful magnetic force on outdoorsy young adults who had turned their recreational preferences into an all-consuming lifestyle that drew nearly theological devotion from its adherents. The town's relatively thin economy might deter families and career-minded singles looking for a place to settle, but it was little barrier to devout nature lovers who could weather the comparatively high cost of living with trust funds, shared apartments or semi-permanent campsites along forest roads. And so, year-by-year, Flagstaff saw a growing influx of wilderness devotees who sought to shape the town into a shrine to Mother Earth, and her prophets: Gary Fisher, Mountain Hardwear, The North Face and Patagonia.

Frankly, the trust-fund hippies were easier to deal with than the big-hat and pickup-truck brigade. The old cowboy types were forever trying to drive him out of a job—or into a ditch on more than a few occasions. The growing ranks of tree huggers meant job security for a guy who administered trees.

But this was something different. There was an air of tension among the beads-and-dreadlocks set.

The BLM official crunched something between his teeth. A whiff of mint reached Van Kamp's nose as the official rolled a plastic candy wrapper into a ball between his fingers and tossed it into a garbage pail.

"It's Greenfield's people," the official said. "He's champing at the bit to settle this mess in Sycamore Canyon and get the fire season rolling before the monsoon rains get the forest too wet to burn. He's gathering his people here before sending them out to Fredonia, Payson and the rest of the targets."

"Greenfield … ?" Van Kamp stuttered, remembering his last encounter with the animal-hating prophet.

"How in Hell did he get his people up here so fast?"

The BLM man cleared his throat. He spat the hard candy to the ground where it clattered and rolled into the parking lot. A half-dozen pairs of environmentally conscious eyes immediately bored into the man like death rays of disapproval. He quickly stooped, retrieved his candy and flicked it into the trash.

Relieved of the barrage of glares, the BLM man turned his attention back to his co-conspirator.

"I don't think these people *do* much of *anything* but show up where he tells them to go."

Van Kamp snorted.

"The last bunch he sent our way had to bicycle their way to Flagstaff from Tucson. I don't think this crew did that overnight."

"Well, it's an emergency, don't you know," the BLM man responded. "He probably let them pile into a VW minibus."

Van Kamp sighed and shook his head.

"To have that kind of power over people …"

"Goddamned impressive, isn't it?"

The two men admired the flow of people on the sidewalk, many of them summoned by the whim of their colleague. But there was that escalating energy in the air, a buzz of bottled-up antagonism marinated in wood smoke. The hippies, outwardly part of the same tribe, slowly gravitated into two overlapping clusters on the sidewalk.

"Of course," the BLM man added. "I'm not sure Greenfield's people play well with others. The local hippies may be tree huggers, but Greenfield's people are tree *fuckers*."

In the door of the coffee house across the street, beneath a sign proclaiming the establishment's vegan orientation, a man in baggy shorts and a ratty t-shirt wiped mustard from the strands of his wispy beard. With exaggerated relish, he devoured a large and obviously meat-laden submarine sandwich.

A shout rose up, words were exchanged, and a brief scuffle broke out. The sandwich eater smirked and drifted away.

Van Kamp sagged. He glanced at the BLM official, who just shrugged in reply.

"Shit."

Chapter 52

"Shit," Greenfield said, unintentionally echoing his co-conspirators just a few blocks away. He gazed across a bobbing sea of heads in Heritage Square, punctuated by a few raised fists, and serenaded by a growing chorus of angry voices.

"We don't have time for this crap. I didn't bring our people up here so they can tangle with animal lovers and rednecks." He paused, tugged at his beard and turned to his younger companion.

"You *do* think we could take 'em, don't you?"

Next to him, Happy, who was known as Henry to his parents, tugged at his own, much wispier, beard. He wore leather sandals, cargo pants and a peach-colored button-down shirt with an unidentifiable food stain on the breast pocket—activist business attire, from head to toe. Activist attire, that is, except for the wild curls of red hair that inspired his nickname; Happy the Clown had been a local celebrity in his upscale California suburb to whom the young Henry had borne a startling resemblance.

"Yeah, we could definitely take the animal lovers—they don't get enough protein. But the rednecks ... The Williams refugees are kind of pissed off ..."

Greenfield grunted and scowled.

"Anyway, we don't have time for that crap. We're supposed

to be making *more* pissed-off rednecks. Did the Fredonia team get off OK?"

"Yeah, but some of the others. Well—" Happy stuttered, and then stopped.

Greenfield backed a few steps from two women engaging in a pushing contest. One wore a peasant skirt and might, or might not, be a member of his organization. The other wore blue jeans and a blouse that must have shrunk in the wash. Several times.

Greenfield tugged his companion's sleeve to pull him from harm's way as the woman in the blouse gave an especially hard shove and sent her antagonist flying. A button from the blouse went flying after her.

"'Well' what?"

"Well … some of our people are confused about what we're doing. I mean they're with the program about burning out the towns, and all."

"Yeah? So what's the problem?"

"What's to keep them from rebuilding? Then this is all wasted effort—*risky* wasted effort. I mean, we're all risking getting busted, and it might not do any good. We don't have enough people to force settlement out of the West."

Greenfield sighed.

"That's why our people are so jumpy?"

"Yeah. Well that—and they know we haven't heard back from Bob, Rena and Sam."

Greenfield backed a few more steps away from what was now a full-blown cat fight with a growing crowd of spectators.

"Look, don't worry about Bob, Rena and Samantha. They're doing important work and they can take care of themselves. You remember how Bob took care of the car dealership don't you? And have you ever seen Rena back down from anything?"

The younger man shrugged noncommittally.

"Besides, we're not going to push anybody out ourselves," the older man's voice rumbled. "We just start the fires. The army will push 'em out."

"The army?"

"Cops, FBI, angry social workers, whatever. This is why we joined up with our uniformed friends. We start the fires, Van Kamp and the other pencil-pushers argue that major parts of the West are too dangerous to live in and they get the wheels turning for a big buy-out of private land—dimes on the dollar because it's all cinders anyway."

"Lots of folks aren't going to like that. They might fight back."

Greenfield smiled.

"I'm counting on it. Plenty of feds will have doubts right up until the first asshole shoots at them. Hell, you know what happens when you call a cop a jerk—even when he's being a jerk."

Happy winced and tugged gently at the scarlet fuzz on his chin.

"Yeah. It's like waving a red sheet at a bull."

"That's right. Their brains will shut down and they'll make it a matter of pride to turn this entire state into a wilderness preserve. We'll get our way without doing any heavy lifting past setting the fires."

The younger man held his tongue for a long moment. He watched the fight, which had now picked up two more participants—another hippy and a cop. The Williams girl in the too-tight blouse was holding her own against all-comers.

"None of them are our people are they?" Greenfield asked.

"Uh ... yeah. Two of them."

"Crap. That's no good."

"Bad publicity?"

"They fight like pussies."

"Umm, another question?"

"Yeah?"

"What if nobody shoots at the feds?"

Greenfield pointed to the fight.

"That doesn't seem too likely."

"But if?"

"Well, Hell. You're a good shot, aren't you? We'll make it happen."

The younger man stood open-mouthed for a moment. He snapped his jaw shut, swallowed and vigorously nodded.

Greenfield smiled back. He returned his attention to the fight and winced almost immediately.

"Damn it! Can't any of our people throw a decent punch?"

Chapter 53

At the other end of the crowded square, another argument brewed.

"Hey man," a lounger said, hunched forward on a low concrete wall, waving a giant burrito with one hand. He spoke loudly to be heard above the sound of the cat fight that held Greenfield's attention just yards away. Wrap-around sunglasses hid his eyes and masked his expression, but earnestness dripped from his voice. "Cool your jets. All I said was that the fire is a travesty! It's killing all sorts of wildlife. Think of the animals chased out of their natural habitat!"

Sitting on the same wall close by in a large circle of people, a woman shook her head vigorously. Her hair stuck out in strands under a bicycle helmet.

"You don't get it. The fire can teach people a lesson about messing with nature. It's part of the natural cycle of life, and humans interfere with nature at their own risk. But it also clears out the parasitic mammals so the plants can reproduce in peace and reach their natural potential."

"Hey," chimed in a woman in sandals and a sky-blue windbreaker. "I get what you're saying about fire teaching people a lesson, but people are invaders in nature. Animals are just doing their thing."

"Whoah. You're forgetting that *animals* are aggressors against *plants*. Lots of times they eat plants with no provocation at all."

"Whoah, that's *bullshit*."

"No, she has a point," said a long-haired man wearing cut-off shorts and … well … shorts. "Animals *do* aggress against plants. Plants don't do anything to them. I think that raises a serious moral issue."

"But Venus Flytraps eat animals. That's aggression."

"They eat *bugs*. Are bugs really *animals*?"

"Hey. We all agree that people deserve what they get. Fuck 'em for building in the forest. But to say that animals deserve the same is—"

"You just don't fucking get it."

"Don't curse at me, man." The guy in the sunglasses rose to his feet and threw his burrito across the now-agitated circle. "How can you hate *animals*?"

Yards away, leaning against the brick wall of a building housing a store that sold hiking and camping gear, two men looked on. Both sported well-used blue jeans and equally well-used faces. One wore a cowboy hat that might once have been a specific color, but had long since absented itself from any recognizable part of the spectrum. The other wore a baseball cap with an unreadable logo.

The one in the cowboy hat spat.

"Did those assholes say we deserved to get burned out?"

The fellow in the baseball cap shifted very slightly.

"I think so. I was concentrating on the whole 'animals are good,' 'animals suck' thing, but I'm pretty sure they said they like forest fires 'cause they hurt people."

The two men stood still for a few minutes, watching the nearby debate grow more violent.

"Hell," cowboy hat said. "I think that deserves some ass-kicking."

Baseball cap smiled. It didn't reach his eyes.

"Damned straight."

The two men broke away from the wall and stepped forward.

Just feet away, the woman in the bicycle helmet turned away from the man she'd just punched and wiped at the splattered food on her shirt. Black beans and red sauce dripped from the fabric.

"Fuck! Is this *vegetarian?*"

Chapter 54

"Rena."

The woman gently extended her hands, running her fingers along the wounded ranger's body, stroking his impassive face. She gently bypassed his eyes, which stared blankly at the sky.

"Rena."

Her fingers moved back down his body, over his chest, to his stomach. Slowly, her fingertips disappeared under the tattered remnants of his loincloth.

"Rena!"

"Oh, I'm sorry. I was just making sure Ray is comfortable."

Jason grunted. Next to him, Samantha giggled.

"Yeah. I think Ray is pretty comfortable. Why don't we all leave him alone so he can get some rest?"

"Wow," Terry said. He stared at Rena and Ray. "That's some first aid."

Bob snickered. The sound became a groan as he jarred his injured shoulder.

"Let's go folks!" He glanced at the sky. "It's getting dark. It's a great time to make camp. Why don't we scatter so we don't give anybody a big target to aim at?"

Terry met his eyes.

"Why don't we get the hell out of here and give them even less of a target?"

Jason pointed at Ray.

"Oh. Yeah."

Moments later, after a few tugs and nudges from Jason—and one longing backwards look by Rena—the teammates scattered into the darkening brush to seek individual refuges for the night. Or, if they preferred, they sought a refuge suitable for two.

Which is what Jason and Samantha did, a few hundred yards up the canyon, back the way they'd come.

"Wow," Samantha said. She brushed Jason's cheek with her hand. "Even when things are tough, you really take charge."

"Thanks." Jason took a tentative half step closer to Samantha, gazing past her dirt-encrusted cheekbones into her moist, welcoming eyes. "I take my responsibilities seriously ... *very* seriously."

She pressed closer to him, and now he felt her nipples tracing little circles through the film of salt, sweat and dust on his chest. The days on the trail with little water and plenty of sweat had taken their toll on her hygiene, creating an almost palpable wall of funk around her—a moat of BO. Now he was inside that wall with her—and she was inside his matching perimeter of stink.

"I never thought I could feel this way about a mammal," she babbled. "And people are just mammals, right?" She broke eye contact with him. "But you're better than just another nasty animal. You're like ... like ... a mighty oak towering above the forest."

Slowly, Jason brought his hands forward and gently rested them on her hips. He raised his right hand to her chin and tilted her head up. Her gaze met his once again.

"And you, you're like a wild doe running free through the forest. You're *my* doe—I hope."

"From you—*only* from *you*—that's so wonderful. Yes, I'm

your doe."

An instant later they were locked in a clinch, lips pressed together. An instant after that, they fell to the ground with a soft thump, which was rapidly punctuated by suppressed yelps as exposed flesh encountered sharp thorns.

Samantha sat up, holding twin branches by the side of her head like a pair of antlers. The two giggled and lurched together again in an embrace.

Yards away, standing half-concealed in the brush, Terry gaped in open astonishment. His jaw opened and closed as if he were trying to speak. Finally, it snapped shut and he turned his head from the scene that had occupied his attention.

He moved quietly up the canyon to find a relatively soft and secluded place to sleep. Through the long hours of the night, Terry would be kept company by very confused thoughts. People, plants, animals, people, plants, animals ...

Rena also moved through the night, though with considerably less confusion than her teammate. Stepping quickly from rock to rock and bush to bush, she rapidly outpaced Bob in their hike up the canyon. Looking carefully around her, she began angling across the canyon, and then cut back down, heading back the way she'd come. She passed within scant yards of Terry who, pacing slowly and staring at his feet, continued on his way none the wiser. Rena spared a quick smile for Jason and Samantha wrestling on a mat of reasonably soft vegetation, and then moved on toward her destination.

Ray looked up as she entered the clearing where he lay, near where he was shot. He looked up and groaned.

"Checking on me already?"

Rena pressed a finger to her lips.

"Ssshh. Sort of."

Ray squinted through the half-light.

"What?" he whispered hoarsely.

Rena dropped to her knees next to the wounded man.

"How's your wound?"

"Same as half an hour ago. It hurts like a son of a bitch."

"Ray, I think we both know what's going on here."

The man raised his eyebrows.

"There's a real connection between us. I felt it during our group discussion of sexuality when you emphasized the sexuality of *people*."

Ray managed to blush through his sunburn.

"What?"

"Ssshh." She touched her finger to his lips. "I really felt it while I was healing you."

"You gotta be—"

"Ssshh."

"It was developing between us before, but there's something magical about the healing process. It's built a strong spiritual bond between us."

She dropped her hands to her waist and shimmied out of her shorts. Ray's eyes widened as her enormous breasts bounced from side to side.

"Hey, not to be ungrateful, but I'm injured. I'm really not up–"

"Ssshh.

Rena patted the man's groin. He instinctively tried to cross his legs, then winced and grunted.

"Yeah, you're hurting. That'll have to wait."

Ray nodded vigorously.

Rena patted him again.

"That's OK. I have something else in mind."

With a quick move, she straddled his chest.

Ray's jaw dropped.

She moved forward, over his face, before he could speak.
"That's better."
"Mmmmf."

Chapter 55

At the mouth of Sycamore Canyon, just yards from the Parson's Spring trailhead, Carrie Olsen buttered a slice of bread for an evening snack and wondered if it was too late to get out of her planned hike with Carl. The recent Wisconsin transplant stared off toward the darkening canyon, torn between the thrill she got from exploring the exotic Southwest desert, and the dark expectation that, somewhere along the trail, she was going to have to poke her backpacking companion in the groin with a sharp object.

Adding to her discomfort was the weird incident on the road leading to the trailhead. She and her companion had come across what looked like an escapee from a horror movie. If she'd been driving, she would have turned around and gone home, but she'd surrendered driving duties to her companion for the trip up from Phoenix to the secluded canyon, and he'd simply accelerated past the bizarre spectacle.

The little Subaru rocked behind her, jarring the tailgate that served as her seat. Caught off-guard, Carrie lost her grip on her butter knife, which skittered off into the dirt. She retained her slice of bread only by clutching it to her t-shirt sticky-side in. Sighing, Carrie peeled her snack away from her clothing, briefly considered—and rejected—eating it anyway, and turned to face the source of the disturbance.

That source sat grinning and scratching his head in the open back of the car. His lower half was encased in a sleeping bag, which rested next to Carrie's own empty bag. His upper half was encased in nothing, which helped to explain why Carrie's sleeping bag was empty, and why she nursed doubts about their planned hike into Sycamore Canyon.

"Oh. I thought you were asleep, Carl."

Carl ostentatiously stretched himself, flexing impressively toned muscles rippling under a rich, mocha complexion. He smiled contentedly—and then broke out in a grin when he spotted Carrie's soiled shirt.

"Mmmm. Hot-buttered midwestern girl. My favorite."

Carrie blushed a deep red and broke eye contact.

"Cool your jets, Carl."

"Hey, did I do that? I'm sorry. I didn't realize I was making such a commotion. Here, let me help." He leaned forward, exposing even more muscles and skin to view.

"No!" she yelled. Then, more calmly, "That's all right. I have it."

Carl grinned again.

"I'm just trying to be helpful."

"Yeah. Hey, if you're not going to sleep yet, why don't you put some clothes on and help me— *Wait!* Let me give you some privacy first."

Carrie hopped from the tailgate and strolled away, eyes carefully turned away from Carl's unclad body and hands outstretched for something that could cleanse her buttered shirt and hands. She debated pressing the local vegetation into dishrag service, and then settled for scrubbing her hands in the dirt and wiping down her shirt with a handful of the same. It might not clean anything, but at least her hands didn't feel so sticky.

On this weekday evening, the dead end of the road that served as a trailhead parking area was empty except for Carrie's vehicle. Carl had no regular work schedule, and she'd traded precious vacation days for privacy on the trail. So there was nothing but the fading light to obstruct her view when a suspiciously familiar figure rounded a bend in the road.

"Carl!"

"Hang on a sec, Miss Buttery Goodness."

"Carl, this is important."

He came up beside her, tucking a much-laundered safari-style shirt into his shorts.

"What's up?"

"That guy—"

"Oh shit! Did he walk all this way? I don't see how he did it."

They watched together as the horror-movie escapee from earlier in the day stumbled into view, closing the distance in slow motion, shambling through the growing dark. The club he'd been waving on the road was missing, seemingly traded for a branch tucked under one arm as a crutch.

"Why don't you get back to the car?" Carl suggested.

Carrie retreated a few feet, but only to grab a trekking pole that rested against the vehicle, exiled along with the rest of their gear to make room in the back to sleep. She returned to Carl's side brandishing the pole, its sharp metal tip pointed vaguely toward the approaching figure.

"Hey, buddy. Can we help you?"

The scary man—which is how Carrie now considered him—stopped in front of them. He was filthy and soaked with sweat. She could smell him from ten feet away.

"You're the people who passed me on the road."

"Yeah …," Carrie said. "We didn't know you needed any

help."

"I was bleeding and yelling for you to stop."

"You looked like a maniac," Carl offered. "You still do."

"Bastards."

Carrie bristled and raised the trekking pole.

"I'm sorry—"

"I'm an officer of the law, goddamnit! You do *not* ignore an officer of the law!"

Carrie peered closely, looking past the blood, dust and assorted bumps and bruises.

"Is that a ranger uniform?"

Carl chimed in.

"Is that *your* ranger uniform?"

The scary man waved his crutch, quickly becoming even scarier.

"Whose uniform do you think it is?"

With his free hand, he slapped at the insignia on his shirt.

"I'm with the Park Service."

Carrie squinted.

"That says 'Forest Service.'"

"Shut up!"

There was silence for a moment. Carrie lowered the tip of the pole to the ground and stared at the scary man, trying to avoid eye contact. All his weight came down on the left foot, like a resting crane, with the right one barely in contact with the ground. She wished, desperately, that she were back at her desk just daydreaming about going hiking.

"You two plan on backpacking the canyon?"

Next to her, Carl cleared his throat.

"Yeah."

"Where is your permit?"

"Permit? There's no permit for—"

The scary man—scary ranger, now—screamed.

"Where's your fucking permit?"

"We don't have one."

"I could arrest you right now!"

"I don't really think—"

The scary ranger awkwardly swapped his makeshift crutch to his left hand and dropped his right to his waist, where it rested on the butt of a pistol.

Carl stopped speaking.

"Maybe we should just go," Carrie said. "We could hike some other time."

"Good idea," the scary ranger said. He staggered toward the trailhead. From his pocket, he withdrew a folded piece of paper, which he quickly tacked to the trailhead sign with two pushpins pulled from the same pocket. Barely legible in the gathering dark, it hung limply in place, proclaiming "Trail Closed" in large block letters.

"Is anybody else hiking in the canyon?"

"I don't think so."

"Good. Good." He pointed to the piece of paper. "Nobody, and I mean *nobody*, is to go hiking here without a permit. Do you understand me?"

"Uh. Yeah."

"Good."

The scary ranger gave them a last look, and then stepped out on the dark trail. Immediately, he lost his footing and went tumbling downhill. They heard him curse, and then right himself out of view.

"I'm all right!"

Then the sounds of laborious walking resumed.

Carrie and Carl stood in place for a long moment, looking in the direction the scary ranger had disappeared.

"Want to catch a movie?" Carl finally asked. "I think there's a theater in Cottonwood."

"Yeah, sure," Carrie answered. She barely noticed Carl's hand resting on her ass.

Chapter 56

Scott lay along the edge of the ledge, chin resting on his hands, peering off into space.

"There is some wacky shit going on down there."

Behind him, Rollo sat back against the rocks enjoying the cool evening breeze. His hat brim was tilted down over his eyes.

"How can you see anything?"

"I can't. They're staying out of view and it's getting too dark anyway. But I'm catching snatches of conversation."

"What are they saying?"

"I'm not really sure, but it sounds like they're not getting along very well."

Rollo grunted.

The younger man slid back from the edge and sat up.

"Hey, buddy. I have a question for you."

Rollo lifted his hand to push the hat out of his eyes.

"Uh oh. I don't like the sound of that."

"Thing is, you've been living out here on your own for a lot of years, right?"

"Yeah. So?"

"And that means you've honed your survival skills. You can build shelters, make fires and hunt and gather with the best of 'em, am I right?"

"I guess so. Where are you going with this?"

"What I want to know is … If you're a modern fucking Daniel Boone, how come you're such a lousy shot?"

Rollo shuffled his feet and grumbled.

"I'm not so bad."

"You're terrible. You should have at least hit somebody by *accident*."

Rollo slumped in place.

"Hey. Another question." Scott raised his hand. "How many fingers am I holding up?"

"It's getting dark—"

"It's not that dark. How many fingers?"

Rollo tilted his head forward and squinted.

"Four. Four, damn it!"

Scott laughed out loud.

"I thought so. You can't see a damned thing, can you?"

Rollo sighed. He wiped both hands over his face, drawing the flesh downwards and smoothing the whiskers on his chin.

Scott scratched at the scruffy new growth lining his own jawbone.

"C'mon. You can't see for shit."

"All right. I can't see very well."

"And you weren't going to admit this because …"

"I hate wearing glasses. They look goofy."

Scott let that hang in the air for a long moment.

"How old are you?"

"Oh for Christ's sake. All right, I need glasses."

"That raises another question—"

"Full of fucking curiosity, aren't you?"

"Only when my life is in the hands of my trusty blind scout."

"Fuck you."

"Anyway." Scott shifted sideways to ease the threat posed by a sharp rock to his posterior. It now nestled in less dangerous position, pressed into his right thigh. "If you can't see, how do you hunt?"

Rollo removed his hat from his head with his right hand and punched the crown with his left fist. Now more crumpled, it went back on top of his head.

"Well ... I'm sneaky."

"How's that?"

"As my eyes have gone south on me, I've had to get closer and closer to my dinner-in-waiting to take a shot. I'm pretty good at sneaking up on deer, elk and whatnot."

"No shit?"

"No shit."

Scott sat silently for several moments staring into space. Then he smiled.

"You think armed, naked pyromaniacs might count as 'whatnot'?"

"You mean khaki-shirted—" Rollo stopped speaking as his eyes went wide. He snatched his hat back off his head and slapped it into the ground.

"Crap!"

* * *

Three, maybe four hours later—neither man had a watch—Scott and Rollo carefully retraced their way down the cliff to the canyon floor below. Dim moonlight gave just enough illumination to make the hazards of the trip apparent, without revealing enough of those hazards to ease the way. Rollo led, slowly, working with gravity to drop from handhold to foothold without sending rocks—or human bodies—plummeting down the cliff to alert the enemy below. More agile, but less accustomed to stalking in the dark, Scott followed in the path of the older man. He assumed that any projection that could handle the larger man's weight would hold his as well.

Muscles strained to ease weight from one hold before applying it to the next. The trick wasn't just to climb down safely, but to do so silently—or with as little noise as possible. Sweat broke out on their foreheads and under their shirts, then dried rapidly in the cool night breeze.

Strained nerves stretched the climb into what seemed like hours, but was only ten or fifteen minutes. With their packs left on the ledge above, they wriggled, slid and fell all the way to the ground with a minimum of noise, fuss and blood loss.

Still in the lead, Rollo stepped cautiously along the canyon floor. He felt with his feet for loose stones before taking each step. By this time, Scott could see little more than the silhouette of his friend, making it difficult to follow his lead. He listened closely to whispered instructions, and then did his best to ape the hermit.

Progress was slow as they inched forward, dodging brush, side-stepping stones and generally sneaking their way up-canyon.

The men froze and ducked as something passed closely overhead.

"Owl," Rollo hissed. "Probably."

Minutes later, Scott stubbed his toe and a stone rolled away like it was shot from a cannon. It sent up a clatter that seemed destined to bring the firebugs down on their heads.

Rollo froze ahead on the trail, and the younger man stifled an apology. Instead, he shrugged, not knowing if his companion could even see the gesture.

Gently placed feet ate up ground quickly, and soon they were in territory that they knew had been occupied just hours before. Rollo held up his hand and waved it to slow the younger man. He stepped even more slowly than before. As he had so many times this night, he eased his foot forward and ...

Coming up behind, Scott saw the older man lose his balance. His arms wagged frantically as he pitched backwards, only to be caught by his younger friend just before he crashed to the ground.

"Rena?" said a voice softly in the dark. "Oh no. Not again. Please, not again. C'mon, please let me sleep."

Scott pushed Rollo upright and then lunged forward. He bent and slapped his hand over a dimly seen mouth.

"No. I'm not Rena," he whispered. He dropped his left knee—hard—on the stranger's ribs. "But I do have a few questions for you."

Rollo dropped into place next to him, clamping his hands like vises on the stranger's arms.

"Damn." He sniffed the air, and then leaned closer to the captive. "Do I smell pussy?"

Chapter 57

L ani slept fitfully, tossing and turning through the night in her sleeping bag tucked amongst the brush on the canyon floor. Moonlight cast an eerie glow over the landscape creating what would have been a beautiful scene, except that it was populated just out of sight by phantom maniacs supplied by her own imagination. Every whisper of wind or rattle of a pebble dislodged by night-traveling creatures became a sneaking marauder.

She'd hiked late the previous day, stopping only as the light faded. A cold meal of powdered hummus, rehydrated and rolled in a slightly stale tortilla, served as her dinner, unwilling as she was to light her stove or make a fire that might serve as a beacon to human predators, however far behind they might be. Washed down with warm water, the tortilla and hummus made for a passable meal, spiced by hunger and anxiety.

Champ seemed equally nervous as he dined on bits of salami mixed with his dry kibble. Between mouthfuls he leaned against Lani and whimpered.

A burst of gunfire up the canyon eroded the last of the woman's calm. The sound echoed and faded, offering no hint as to its resolution. She sat on her sleeping mat resting her head on her knees and fearing the worst. With night falling—and Champ pawing sympathetically at her hair—she'd made her camp in as concealed a spot as possible. She drew on years of outdoor experience to choose a small clearing hidden from easy view. A taste for unauthorized backpacking trips in national parks had taught her the basics of concealment. Rocks and shrubs up-canyon from the clearing broke up the ground so as to discourage hikers from tramping through the refuge—or so Lani hoped.

And so she'd made a restless night of it, worrying about Scott, about the gunshots, even—who'd have thought?—about Rollo.

Picking up on her mood, Champ stood guard. He sat upright at the edge of the clearing, staring up-canyon. From time to time he growled softly at unseen menaces and shifted his weight from paw to paw. Lani slept little, but every time she checked, the dog was awake and on-duty.

Morning came as it usually did in canyons, peeking tentatively over the rocky walls and easing itself noncommittally toward the ground below.

Lani had her sleeping bag rolled and stowed with the first splash of sunlight.

"We've been through a lot, Champ, but this is a new one. Maybe we should have a chat with Scott about toning down the amount of adventure in our lives. I could use a little boredom."

Champ whoofed softly. Lani took that as disagreement. She'd often suspected that Champ was a bit of an adrenaline junky.

Staring up-canyon, Lani couldn't help but wonder about the outcome of the previous night's shooting. True, plenty of ammunition had been expended to little effect so far, and the pursuers seemed more of a danger to themselves than to her and her friends, but there was no ignoring the fact that she was the one who was running. The firebugs might not be the most competent bad guys in the world, but they were tough enough to keep Scott, Rollo and herself on the defensive.

"I'm not sure we're as tough as Scott and Rollo think we are," Lani told Champ.

Champ whoofed again. He definitely disagreed.

"You're pretty confident, buddy."

With the sun rising and the situation up the canyon uncertain, it was time to get going. Lani shouldered her pack with difficulty. The weight of the gun on her hipbelt threw her off and she thrashed around before getting the shoulder straps settled and everything snapped and tucked where it belonged. Annoyed though she was by the unaccustomed bulk, the gun was reassuring.

Champ lapped enthusiastically from a stagnant pool of water left nestled in the rocks. He snorted with approval and started down the canyon. Lani sipped from her water tube. Her water supply was low, but she expected to hit Parsons Spring soon and so avoid the need to follow the dog's example.

The sun rose slowly in the sky—or so it seemed as the duo made good time. Lani felt a little safer as she put distance between herself and the pursuing firebugs. Then she felt guilty about her relief as she remembered that Scott and Rollo were back along the trail protecting her retreat.

Even though she had descended in altitude into warmer country, she felt the brush of a slightly cool breeze across her cheek. At the same time, the rocky ground gave way to marsh grass.

"Parson Spring, Champ. Drink your fill."

The dog did just that, pausing to belch wetly as Lani filled her water bladder.

"Thanks, buddy," she said as she returned the bladder to her pack. "Try aiming the other way next time."

Now she followed an actual trail, marked by cairns, along the creek that trickled away from the spring. She could almost feel a shower at the end of the trail. Yeah, a shower, followed by a cold drink to wash down a decent meal. There had to be somebody along the trail or at the trailhead. Even if there wasn't anybody there, there were a few isolated houses and maybe campers along the road leading to Clarkdale. She'd get help soon enough.

Lost in her thoughts as she was, Lani didn't hear the man approaching through the brush. She just sensed Champ stiffening next to her. And then the dog growled.

Surprised, she looked up to see ... Christ! Who in Hell is that?

Ahead was a ragged cripple in a torn and filthy ranger uniform, hobbling along with a branch tucked in place as a crutch.

If Yellowstone is still staffed after World War III, Lani thought, that's who'll be working the visitors center.

And then the man reached for his gun.

Chapter 58

Tim awoke by the bank of Sycamore Creek to a chorus of aches and pains. The worst irritation emanated from his mangled fingertip, which glowed an angry red in the early morning light. He inserted the finger into his mouth, alternately sucking and chewing it to relieve a bit of the pain.

But the throbbing resumed immediately once he removed the digit from his mouth.

"Oh fuck," he groaned.

Stiff from pain and from a night spent on the ground, the battered ranger slowly crawled from his sleeping bag and popped his head out of the cramped, one-person tent. He took in a deep breath of air that didn't smell like ... well ... badly aged *Tim*.

Everything else might have gone wrong, he told himself, but at least he'd packed enough gear to get through the night. He hadn't had a car wreck and personal injuries in mind when he'd set out from Flagstaff, but he'd had no intention of emulating that idiot Jason's lack of planning skills either. He had no doubt that his colleagues up the canyon were having a miserable time of it, if they hadn't already been led to their doom by the idiot.

Tim Vasquez was prepared for *anything*.

Without thinking, he stretched and yawned. That stressed

various components of his right ankle that were no longer up to the task of bearing much abuse at all. He winced and cursed again. The cursing escalated until he unleashed an inarticulate scream that echoed through the canyon.

Taking a deep breath, Tim calmed himself. Then he spoke clearly, enunciating each word distinctly.

"I. Am. A. Law. Enforcement. Officer."

He felt better. He felt official. The uniform—what was left of it—represented the authority of the Park Service behind him. The weight of the gun on his hip embodied the power the Park Service wielded through him.

And all was right with the world.

Except that certain parts of his body still hurt really bad.

Screw this. It was time to get the day started.

Starting late as he had, and hobbling as he was, Tim hadn't made it far along the trail after his encounter with the hiking couple at the trailhead.

"Fucking yuppies," he muttered, remembering the pair.

He'd made his camp along Sycamore Creek, well below Parson Spring. The water flowed free and cold here, so he bathed his wounds and his clothes as best he could. The dust and sweat rinsed away, but bloodstains and rips permanently marred the fabric of his uniform.

Checking his reflection in a still pool, Tim decided that he was as presentable as possible under the circumstances. It was time to check in. He grabbed his cell phone and eyed the screen for a signal. He smiled. The signal was weak, but he was happy to be able to use the phone at all.

He dialed a pre-set number.

"Chief Ranger Van Kamp? This is Ranger Vasquez. I just want to let you know—

"What?

"No, I'm just heading up the canyon–

"Why? Because I ran into some trouble with the truck—

"No, it's *not* still running. It's totaled.

"Hello?"

Tim pulled the cell phone from his ear and stared at it for a long moment. He briefly considered calling Van Kamp again, but dropped the idea.

"Weird little elf," he muttered. He tucked the phone back into his pocket.

With the sun rising in the sky, Tim shouldered his pack and his makeshift crutch and started—slowly—up the trail. He whistled a marching tune he'd learned on late-night TV—something from a movie about British POWs during World War II. He admired their plucky spirit and their sense of duty.

He thought again of his odd conversation with Van Kamp.

"Why'd he get so damned upset about the truck?"

But the answer to his question wouldn't be found here.

On he hobbled. The many creek crossings stumped him at first. Wet, moss-covered stepping stones provided poor traction for his lame ankle and crutch. He feared a fall that would add to his already painful litany of injuries. In the end, he settled for wading through the shallow water at each crossing, trusting to the creek bottom to provide firmer footing then the stones.

After the first crossing, his feet were thoroughly soaked, so his hike was now serenaded by a creaky squishing sound from his hiking boots.

Heavy with water, his boots slowed him further.

Along a dry stretch of trail, he turned a bend in the cliff face. A small opening in the canyon wall looked to him like an abandoned wildcat mine. He stopped for a drink of water and surveyed the area. Scattered remnants of rusting mining equipment in the brush confirmed his guess. He wondered what had drawn the long-gone miners to this canyon. Arizona was known as a copper state, but almost anything could have drawn a wandering prospector's attention.

Then he snickered as he thought of how his allies Bob, Rena and Samantha would react to the abandoned mine. Greenfield's fanatics wouldn't like this intrusion into their church, he guessed.

"Somebody shit on their altar," he said out loud.

He snickered again—and then stopped, abruptly, as another sound caught his attention.

Somebody was coming down the trail. Whoever it was must have been quiet because they were close and they—*she*. There she was! A cute, if slightly grubby, blonde came into view, backpack in place and eyes on the ground before her. She was alone except for a black-and-white dog trotting ahead.

Tim flushed. His breath quickened.

He recognized that dog from the confrontation up on the rim. Mottled black and white with a prominent dark spot on top of its head, that dog was with the guy who'd spied on Jason and his team and disappeared into the canyon—very likely with incriminating evidence.

And if the dog had been on the rim, he bet the woman had been there too.

He reached for his pistol.

"You! Hey you there!"

Chapter 59

"What kind of bird is that?" Jason wondered softly into Samantha's ear. Something warbled again, an oddly familiar sound, but one he couldn't place in distance or origin.

The two environmental crusaders—Jason had tentatively settled on the idea that he and his team were crusaders, though the thought brought up mental images at least as troubling as those associated with his musings about Carthage—lay nestled side by side in their chosen haven near the canyon wall. Thick brush gave them privacy, creating the illusion of a private love nest. Well, a somewhat less-than-luxurious private love nest that was already, early in the morning, growing uncomfortably warm.

"I'm not sure," Samantha mumbled. Her eyes were closed and her head rested on Jason's arm, bringing her lips within a scant few inches of his own. "It sounds like—"

Her eyes flew open. She lifted her head from Jason's arm and listened carefully.

"It sounds like somebody crying."

Jason lifted his own head.

"Huh." He was still for a long moment. "It does sound like somebody crying. It's probably Terry—"

"It's not me," came a voice from a nearby bush. "I'm not the one who's crying."

"Crap." Jason reached for his shorts and scrambled into them without rising from the ground.

"You're so modest," Samantha giggled. She ran her fingers through her hair, dislodging twigs and other bits of vegetation. Then she shook her head, flipping her curls around her face and setting other parts of her anatomy into motion.

Jason looked on in awe. Then he shook his own head.

"I'm not that modest," he whispered. "Terry just creeps me out a little."

"That's cold," Terry answered. His head popped into view through the brush. "And it's uncalled for."

Samantha paused in mid-groom.

"Have you been there all night?"

Terry's mouth hung open, and then snapped shut abruptly.

"Not *all* night."

"That's what I'm talking about, Terry," Jason said. "That's just not right."

Terry's face seemed to sag.

"I was just a little ..." his voice trailed off.

Without turning her back, Samantha wriggled into her shorts. The view set off a biological response in Jason that had him happy he was already dressed. Well, half-dressed.

"Hey," Samantha said. "I think somebody *is* crying."

With the topic of conversation mercifully changed, the trio set off down the canyon. It wasn't hard to follow the sound since it meant little more than retracing their steps of the evening before. With daylight creeping into the canyon, they easily made their way back to the clearing in which Ray had been left to spend the night.

There, they found Bob and Rena struggling to free the wounded Park Ranger, who was bound hand and foot. A scrap of filthy fabric lay crumpled by the man's head. Bob fumbled at the restraints with just his uninjured arm and made slow progress as a result.

"What the fuck?" Jason said. "What happened here?"

"I don't know," Rena answered. She glanced briefly toward the team leader but wouldn't meet his eyes. "He was like this when we found him. He started crying as soon as we got the gag out of his mouth."

"Didn't anybody guard him?"

Bob shrugged.

"You kind of suggested that we all leave him alone." He glanced at Rena who kept here eyes firmly fixed on a stubborn knot. "I guess we all thought he'd be safe enough by himself."

"Crap."

Terry and Samantha joined the effort to free Ray while Jason looked around the clearing for clues as to the night's events. The clearing was small and bare except for Ray's backpack, so he soon gave up the effort and returned to his wounded comrade.

"Ray, buddy."

The man continued weeping.

"Ray, I need to know what happened."

The man stopped crying.

"Jason, it was fucking horrible."

The team leader caught a flash of motion from the corner of his eye. He turned to see Rena staring straight down at the ground. What little of her face was visible was bright red. Confused, Jason turned back to Ray.

"What was horrible?"

"I was tortured."

Rena looked up.

"Tortured?"

"Well, sort of tortured."

"What do you mean?" Jason asked.

"The big guy sat on me until I talked."

"Sat on you? Wait. What big guy?"

Ray met his gaze. His face looked blank, worn out.

"The people we're chasing. Two of them. I don't know if there are any more. Anyway, they came down during the night, found me and questioned me. Then they tied me up. It was horrible." He grabbed Jason's arm and pulled him closer. "I held out on the most important information. I never told them about Tim."

Rena gently brushed Ray's forehead.

"Oh, you poor thing."

Ray shuddered, but said nothing.

Jason opened his mouth to speak, but thought better of it. He looked around the clearing again and spotted Ray's backpack. By itself.

"Ray, where's your rifle."

"What? It should be over there." He pointed.

"It's not there. Shit."

They all ducked as the first gunshot of the morning sounded—directly overhead.

Chapter 60

With a snarl, Champ raced forward before Lani had fully digested the situation. The ragged ranger yelled, and Lani opened her mouth to call off the dog—why was her big, friendly pooch attacking a ranger?—when an important fact registered in her mind: the battered, odd-looking ranger had a rather nasty-looking firearm in his hand.

"*Oh.* I guess Rollo was right. What are the chances of that?"

The ranger hopped in place on one foot, having dropped the branch that served as his crutch, and raised the pistol away from the holster on his hip.

The dog closed the gap, paws a blur against the ground, muscles rippling beneath his dirty fur. Dust exploded in spurts from the contact of his claws on the ground and rose in a haze that hung in the air.

Lani grabbed for her own pistol. Unpracticed, she fumbled at the holster's thumb break, losing a precious second before the snap parted and her hand slid down over the grip, grating against checkered wood panels and reaching for the trigger.

The ranger's gun came up toward Lani, its bore tracing a line up her torso. She felt—she *imagined* she felt—a fiery dot move across her flesh, as if a powerful laser beam projected from the gun's muzzle. She braced for the impact of the expected bullet.

Like the anchor of a boat, Lani's gun weighed down her hand as she dragged it from her holster and raised it into position. Remembering lessons taught by Scott, her fingers wrapped around the grip and depressed the safety, her left hand rose to support her right hand. In her mind was the certain knowledge that she was losing the race with the homicidal ranger.

Within feet of the stranger, Champ hunched his muscles to cross the final gap with the interloper. The ranger's eyes flickered, recognizing the new threat. The muzzle of his gun wavered.

Lani wrestled to bring her gun into position, fighting gravity and feeling every ounce of steel in the pistol's composition. She wasn't moving fast enough.

Champ leaped.

The ranger fired.

The dog struck with a dull sound, like a mallet hitting meat. The ranger's mouth opened wide in surprise. He grunted. Two bodies fell in a tangle of fur and flesh.

Champ lay still and broken like a discarded toy. His body stretched out, half on the ground, his lower half resting on the ranger's chest. The dog's blood puddled on the hard-packed dirt of the trail.

"*Nooo!*" Lani screamed.

Cursing, the ranger pushed the dead dog aside, and rose to a sitting position. His gun remained clenched in his hand.

Lani brought her pistol into position. The front sight lined up in the notch of the rear sight, against the ranger's chest. She fired.

Once.

Twice.

The gun bucked hard after each shot, defying gravity and her strength to rise toward the sky.

The ranger sprawled backward, his gun tumbling from his

hand to rest in the dirt.

Sobbing, Lani ran to the dog. She had to step over the body of the man to reach the animal, and saw his eyes, wide and staring up at the sky. He had already done all the harm he would ever do. She dropped her gun to the ground and grabbed hold of the remains of her pet.

Champ's body lay warm and dusty as she cradled his head in her lap. She sat in place, crying and holding the dog as the sun rose higher in the sky.

Eventually—how much later, she didn't know—she rose from the ground and slapped sensation back into her legs, which had cramped during her period of mourning. She dropped her backpack to the ground. With great effort, she dragged the dog's body into the brush. Using only her hands, she dug a shallow grave into which she placed Champ. Dirt caked under her fingernails and blood oozed from small cuts as she pushed aside thorns and sharp stones. Finally, she piled rocks over the body to protect it as best she could from scavengers.

Rising once again, she returned to the trail where the ranger lay staring sightlessly at the sky, his mouth still open in a wide "O." Without a word, she retrieved her pistol from the ground and returned it to the holster. Then she leaned forward over the prone figure and spat. The glob made a star pattern on the dead man's forehead.

Permitting herself one final sob, Lani donned her pack and continued along the trail.

Chapter 61

A whiff of smoke hung in the air. The whir of the fan in the window suddenly changed in tone. The blade visibly turned slower, and then slower still.

Van Kamp sighed.

"Power's out," the Park Service man said. "Again."

"That's the least of it," Van Kamp said. "People in Flagstaff are used to losing power during the monsoon. But riots are new. Those draw attention we don't need."

"Especially when it turns downtown into a smoking war zone," The Park Service man muttered.

"True," Van Kamp allowed. "The news cameras love that."

"Cops are all over the place," The BLM man said. He peered through the motel room window above the now-dead fan at Route 66 outside. "So are some of your trucks." He glanced at his pint-sized colleague perched on a chair near the dark television.

"I loaned personnel to the Flagstaff police—the ones who aren't heroically fighting the forest fire." Van Kamp said. He chuckled—an abrupt, nervous sound. "It was the least we could do to help a sister agency suppress the hoodlum element."

"S-m-a-a-a-r-t," the BLM official said. "Great way to distance yourself from Greenfield's people. I'll send some of mine, too."

"Even better," the Park Service man muttered," if your guys *shoot* some of Greenfield's people. That'll give you plenty of distance."

Van Kamp giggled again.

"So you've had it with Greenfield?"

"Haven't you? Isn't that why we're meeting in this roach motel?"

The BLM official stepped away from the window.

"Damned straight it is. We've got rednecks from Williams hunting college kids through the streets of Flagstaff. Tree-huggers are pounding on animal lovers when they're not dodging the cowboys. And a perfectly good downtown Chinese restaurant is a smoldering ruin because, depending on who you ask, they murdered animals or slaughtered plants."

"I think it was torched just because it was there," Van Kamp said. He sighed again. "I'll miss their potstickers. Pork and vegetable both."

The Park Service man snorted.

"It won't matter why the place got burned if we get linked to it, and that's a distinct possibility with that fiasco in Sycamore Canyon. We need to leave Greenfield and his fanatics holding the bag on this one."

Van Kamp hopped from his chair and landed gently on the floor. He began to pace.

"I think we can do better than that. I mean, if the joint task force—headed by those present—successfully exposes a dangerous ring of criminals threatening the public lands, we'll be in a nice position. I think we can get a fair share of extra funding and increased resources. I don't think we can tag Greenfield as an Arab, but he's a pretty easy sell as a terrorist of some kind or other."

"Oh, I like that."

"I mean, terrorism is a threat to the American way of life."

The Park Service man frowned.

"I don't think an incarcerated Greenfield is going to keep our secrets very well. He can get us in hot water if we hang him out to dry."

The BLM official whistled softly and glanced at the spotty ceiling. He grimaced at the sight.

"Dead men tell no tales."

"Even better," Van Kamp said. "A martyred Greenfield might just inspire his followers to continue the fight and keep us in business for years to come."

The Park Service man slapped himself in the forehead.

"Of course! Silly me. He's going to resist arrest, right?"

The fan in the window began spinning once again.

Chapter 62

N ot far away, Greenfield shared his colleagues' assessment of their best interests—though he was somewhat less approving of where that assessment led.

"Those seat-warmers are going to hang us out to dry," he told Happy, who nervously chewed the end of his whiskers while being led across the asphalt parking lot by a firm grip on his right arm. "I'll bet on it. They don't have the balls to tough it out through a little social disorder. Hell, what did they think was going to happen after we set those fires? We *want* social disorder."

Greenfield spoke loudly, but his resonant voice was wasted on a one-man audience in the otherwise empty lot south of the railroad tracks that ran through Flagstaff's downtown. The social disorder that Greenfield celebrated had taken an expensive toll on the city's usual shopping and tourist trade.

"Uh huh," Happy said. "Yeah. Social disorder is good."

The older man paused to turn and glare.

Happy's face flushed.

"Really! I agree. We want people to move along and realize that it's not worth living here."

Greenfield nodded and continued on his journey with his sidekick in tow.

"That's right! We don't want people settling here, trampling grass and cutting down trees—*beautiful* trees. And if it takes a little social disorder to do the trick, then that's what it'll..." he trailed off, a puzzled look on his face.

Hoping to improve his standing in the older man's eyes, Happy jumped in.

"Then we'll cheerfully cause a little social disorder."

The older man rocked his head, thinking.

"Sure. Why not?"

The journey across the parking lot ended at a mud-spattered jeep that looked as if it had been purchased as surplus after enduring hard duty in the motor pool of some Third-World army. Rust welded the doors shut—an obstacle that Greenfield bypassed by clumsily climbing in the passenger side, leg up and over.

Happy stood awkwardly in place until his indecision drew notice.

"Well, don't just stand there, damn it, drive." Greenfield shook a set of keys in the air so they jingled, and then tossed them for Happy to catch.

Happy followed the other man's example, hopping into the driver's seat.

"Where to?"

"Sycamore Canyon."

Happy gaped even as he started the engine. He cranked it once, twice, and then it caught.

"Why?"

The older man smirked.

"Our allies may want to hang us out to dry, but they can't if there's no way to link us to the fires. The only people not involved in our plans who can actually do that—who actually have photos of our people setting fires—are down in Sycamore Canyon."

Happy pressed the clutch down to the floor and jerked hard

on the gearshift. He backed the jeep out of its parking space, hit the brake and stalled the vehicle.

Greenfield glared in silent disgust.

Happy restarted the engine and eased the jeep onto empty West Phoenix Avenue, and then to sparsely traveled South Milton.

"So, what are we going to do at Sycamore Canyon?"

Greenfield smirked again.

"We're going to get rid of the evidence, of course. They can't come after us without evidence."

"You mean the pictures?"

"And the people who took the pictures. Do I really have to spell it out for you?

Happy felt less suited to his nickname than ever before. Maybe he should go back to his given name. Henry wasn't all that bad. Maybe even Hank. No, he couldn't pull off Hank. But Henry was acceptable.

The older man barked an interruption to Happy's line of thought.

"And Jesus Christ, take it easy on that clutch."

Chapter 63

"I s-e-e-e y-o-o-o-u," Rollo yelled over the edge of the new ledge.

Well, strictly speaking, the ledge wasn't new; it had been in place for thousands of years, changed only by the slow erosion of wind and rain, and the comparatively quicker gropings of plant roots into crevices in the rock. As far as Scott and Rollo were concerned, however, it was a new perch chosen in the dark as a replacement for their abandoned station.

Somewhat more precarious than its predecessor, the ledge sloped toward its edge at a slight angle that promised anybody seeking a resting place a continuing wrestling match with gravity.

It wasn't an ideal location by any means. Aside from its slope, it was also exposed to sun, wind and rain. It had one important advantage over the previous ledge, however: it provided an excellent view of the firebugs below and of their escape routes both up and down the canyon.

As Rollo leaned out to heckle the people below, Scott lounged in place, taking advantage of the ledge's angle to recline in relative comfort with a view of the sky above.

"Just so you know, Rollo," the younger man said in a low voice. "You look pretty close to the tipping point to me."

If you fall over, there's no way I can haul your fat ass back up and also fight off the firebugs."

Rollo grunted, and then continued his soliloquy.

"I want to thank you sons of bitches for the gift of this fine automatic rifle. I promise to be a better shot with it than any of you."

"Oh, this was a mistake," Scott muttered. He scrambled to change position and carefully shimmied forward on his belly with the ancient British rifle in his hand. He peered over the edge.

Filthy, half-naked and, by all appearances, utterly dejected, the firebugs stood below. Four of them looked reasonably healthy, if not happy. One stood with his right arm held in place by an improvised sling that looked dirtier than his bare skin. The sixth firebug—dressed only in a tattered, silvery loincloth—lay quietly with his face covered by his crossed arms.

If he had to guess, Scott figured the prone man to be the one he and Rollo had questioned during their nocturnal raid.

"I got it under control," Rollo whispered.

Scott ignored his companion's protest.

"What my friend means is that we're tired of being chased and shot at. We've sent the video we took of you setting the forest fire ahead. Since the evidence is already well beyond your reach, why don't you sit still and play nice until help comes? You can start by stacking your weapons directly below us."

"Oh," Rollo said. "Good idea."

Not all of the firebugs agreed. Through loud shushing from one of his companions, the man with his arm in a sling defiantly shouted back.

"Fuck you. Nobody— Back off, Terry. Nobody— I mean it. Grow a spine, Terry. Nobody is coming to help you."

Genuinely puzzled, Scott asked the inevitable question.

"Oh? Why's that?"

With a triumphant look on his face, the mud- and dust-spattered gimp replied.

"Because when all this started, we sent somebody for help. By now they're at the mouth of the canyon. Whoever you sent is probably dead. So why don't *you* surrender to *us*?"

Without moving, the man on the ground let out a loud groan.

"It wasn't my idea!" somebody—apparently Terry—yelled.

"Wimp."

"Grow a spine."

"Where are your balls?"

For his part, Scott sighed and turned to Rollo.

"I know," Rollo said. "I can hold these assholes here. Which gun do you want?"

Chapter 64

"Way to go, Terry."

His face glowing red, the scrawny ranger stared at his feet. He declined to respond to any of the catcalls of his colleagues.

Staring at the ledge above, and the barely visible faces at the promontory's edge, Jason broke in.

"I'm less concerned about Terry's spinelessness—"

"Hey!"

"—than I am about Bob's revealing that Tim went for help."

Bob's eyes widened.

"Huh?"

"It looks like two people are up there. What if one of them heads down the canyon and shoots whoever Van Kamp sent?"

"That leaves one guy here watching us. He has to sleep eventually."

"Yeah ... eventually. In the meantime we're stuck here."

A voice drifted down from above.

"You heard the man! Stack your damn guns below me, goddamnit!" The command was punctuated by a gunshot, immediately followed by the whine of a bullet speeding down the canyon.

Hopping to comply, Rena dragged her rifle by the muzzle.

She tossed it into a bush, from which it slid to the ground with a clatter.

"Did you hear what he said?"

"Yeah," Jason answered, irritated. "I'm getting my rifle already."

"That's not what I mean. He said they sent the *video* up ahead."

"Huh?"

"We might have argued that photos were taken out of context, but video will be a clincher."

Jason stood dumb for a long moment. Then he sighed.

"This just gets better and better."

Standing at his side, Samantha rested a hand on his arm, but said nothing.

Jason sighed again.

"Shit. This is why I hate technology."

Chapter 65

S tep after plodding step, Lani climbed the steep path to the
trailhead. Hot, sweaty work, it was an accomplishment, but a
small one. Miles of empty, unpaved road awaited her unless
somebody was parked at the trailhead. She'd seen nobody but the
crazed ranger on the trail, so she prepared herself for an extended
hike.

Lurking in the back of her mind, pushed there by conscious
effort, was the memory of Champ shot and lying in the dirt. As her
self-appointed guardian and constant companion, the dog had
earned her love and respect. Champ had placed himself in harm's
way more than once to protect his mistress, and she knew his loss
would hurt even when the memory was no longer fresh.

As for the dead ranger … Fuck 'im.

Maybe she should feel remorse for shooting the man, but she
felt only satisfaction. The ranger was an arsonist and had threatened
Lani and her friends even before he'd shot Champ. Killing him
couldn't bring Champ back, but it protected her own life. It even,
she felt, balanced the scales a bit for the death of the dog.

She'd had a cell phone signal—however tentative—for a
while, now, and she'd considered following Scott's instructions for
uploading the video from the phone. But the rest of his

plan—specifically, the mailing list of journalists—required a computer, and she felt more comfortable at a keyboard than picking her way through a smart phone with her thumbs anyway.

She'd also considered calling for help, but who? It was tough enough *before* she shot the ranger. So far as she knew, the Forest Service had jurisdiction out here, with maybe some input from the county sheriff's department. Calling the Forest Service to complain about homicidal, naked Forest Service employees running amok struck her as a risky venture at best. Calling *any* law-enforcement agency after she'd plugged a psycho in a uniform smacked of suicide. Cops might have their intrafamilial spats, but she had no doubt that, like members of a dysfunctional family, they'd close ranks very quickly against an outsider who'd proven a quicker shot than one of their own, however deranged that one had been.

No, she couldn't risk calling for help until the video was in public view.

The trailhead sign came into view, and with it, the possibility of assistance for her mission. Summoning her reserves, Lani pushed her way up the last few steps and discovered that she had company. Two large people—a man and a woman—stood in place studying a piece of paper tacked to the trail sign. They were dressed in matching straw cowboy hats, collared western-style denim shirts and blue jeans.

"Closed?" the man asked, tugging at the brim of his hat. "Why is the trail closed?"

The woman next to him shrugged. Her face was hidden in shadow under her own hat, but she seemed as puzzled as her companion.

The man turned to Lani as she stepped out past the sign.

"Was the trail closed when you went in?"

Lani shook her head.

"What? I don't think so. There's no reason for the trail to be closed." She stopped speaking as she saw the hand-lettered sign. Her mouth dropped open, and then snapped shut.

"Oh. I bet that was put there by the ranger I shot."

She caught herself.

"Oh shit. I know how that sounds. I mean he deserved it because he shot my dog and was part of a gang of crazy arsonists."

The large couple stared. The man scratched at his jaw. The woman twirled a canteen by its canvas strap.

"Umm … " Lani said. "I'm not really presenting this right, am I?"

"Well," the man said, worrying again at the brim of his hat. "The part about shooting a ranger might put most folks off, but we like to think of ourselves as open-minded. Why don't you start from the beginning?"

Chapter 66

Desperate as he was to reach Lani, Scott knew he had to move carefully. Rather than drop down to the canyon floor and risk a confrontation with the firebugs below, he climbed to the top of the mesa to find a trail that paralleled the lower trail and intercepted it near the trailhead. Rollo had used the higher trail when he'd buried his cache, and he said it was an easier hike than the canyon floor.

Of course, *easier* was a relative term. By the time he made it to the mesa's top, he was already out of breath. Scrapes oozing blood marred his forearms and a spot on his left shin promised to swell and turn purple.

He then lost precious minutes following game traces and meandering tracks stamped by grazing cattle. Each path started out promisingly before wandering in circles and then petering out—or forking into multiple trails.

One promising lead faded, only to be followed by another, and another—each ending in a cactus, a cliff or a mess of hoof prints left by cattle seemingly as confused as he was himself.

Panic had begun to set in when he stumbled on a cairn marking the true trail. A small pile of rocks left by hikers, rangers or cattlemen, its sight removed a huge burden from Scott's shoulders. Once the first cairn was spotted, the next followed in short order.

From then on he hopped from cairn to cairn, following the stones through the desert as if they were breadcrumbs.

The hours passed in a blur. Despite his best intentions, his pace slackened. The sun was high, the day was hot, and he had few reserves left after the chase through the canyon.

Scott bypassed a muddy bowl in the ground even though his pack grew lighter with each sip taken from the drinking tube. The water was brown, opaque with dirt stirred up by the dumb beasts cooling themselves in the liquid. He wasn't yet out of water, and was far from thirsty enough to be tempted by the cow shit-tainted muck.

The sound of a shot in the distance sent an almost electric surge through his body.

It came from ahead, down in the canyon. Yes, echoes could deceive, but he was sure the sound came from ahead.

He was already sprinting when two more shots rang out, but he couldn't maintain the pace. The breath caught in his throat and his pack swayed on his back. He settled into a trot. Air hissed in and out of his mouth as he stifled gasps.

The trail here was better delineated than it had been earlier. While not exactly much-traveled, it had seen enough use over the years to wear an ankle deep scar in the landscape.

At last, the trail began to trend downward. Despite a stitch in his side, he maintained a trot wherever the trail allowed for quick passage. Sweat poured from his skin and pasted his shirt to his body. His left hand, clasped around the light-weight stock of the .22, had passed beyond pain and grown numb.

At Sycamore Creek he paused long enough to scoop water in double-handfuls into his mouth, and then over his head.

On the far side of the creek, he had a decision to make. Here, the trail forked. The right-hand path led upwards toward the trailhead; the left-hand path doubled back where he'd come from.

Trusting to instinct, Scott turned left. If Lani is in trouble, he reasoned, she'd be farther back on the trail, held up by the missing firebug. If she's *still* in trouble, a treacherous voice in his head said. He did his best to ignore the gibe.

He was still in a frenzy sometime later when he rounded a bend in the trail and nearly stumbled over a corpse.

The first impression that struck Scott—aside from shock at the discovery of a body in the middle of a hiking trail—was that the corpse looked surprised. A look of open-mouthed astonishment had survived the unlucky fellow.

Scott prodded the stiff with the barrel of the .22 rifle.

Yes, he was very dead.

The second impression that struck him was that the dead man appeared to have been ill-used even before his untimely death. His ranger uniform was torn and grubby, and he had several obvious injuries that seemed to pre-date his demise. Scott rifled the man's pockets and found a Park Service law-enforcement badge to match the Sig in the dirt. It was an interesting contrast to the Forest Service uniform, but Scott mentally filed it away as just a minor item in several days of weirdness.

Carefully, eyes straying again and again to the body on the ground, Scott searched the area for clues to what happened. In short order, he discovered an odd pile of stones. Soon after, he uncovered the body of Champ.

"Oh, Lani," he groaned. "Well, of course a cop would shoot a dog. Good for you for shooting back."

He quickly restored Champ's makeshift grave, and then sprinted back up the trail the way he'd come.

Chapter 67

"Thank you *so* much," Lani gushed. "I can't tell you what a relief it was to run into somebody at the trailhead. After what we've been through … It's just … are you sure it's OK with you that I use your computer?" She knew she was babbling, but she couldn't help herself. The words streamed out in a torrent, uncorked by her relief at meeting people who didn't want to shoot at her.

"Not a problem," Bill McGinty answered from the driver's seat of his dusty pickup truck. "That might be a small screen on that phone of yours, but I know what I saw. We're happy to be of help. Are you sure you don't want to go to the hospital or the police before you do anything else?"

In the rear left jump seat, Lani vigorously shook her head.

"No. That man back there was a ranger and one of my friends is convinced the Forest Service is behind this. If he's right, the cops may not be of any help."

"You know that's true, Bill," Emma chimed in. "Those uniformed types can be a tight bunch." She turned in the shotgun seat and shot the younger woman a wink. "We've had our own run-ins with the law."

"Oh?"

Bill chuckled.

"To hear some folks tell it. We're regular public enemies."

The McGintys laughed uproariously.

Bounced from side to side in the jump seat, Lani mentally filed the mysterious private joke for later attention, once she'd fully processed the events of the past few days. She had enough to worry about now without prying into the private lives of her rescuers.

"We'll have to call the police at some point," Emma continued. "But let's get done what you need to get done first."

As the truck rumbled down the long dirt road leading away from Sycamore Canyon, Lani caught sight of a wrecked Park Service truck by the side of the road. She wondered if it had any connection to the ranger she'd met on the trail, then promptly forgot the matter.

Chapter 68

Scott took the last 100 yards of the trail at a pace much slower than the sprint he intended. The trail climbed steeply uphill here and was terraced in places with rough steps to ease the passage of hikers. The steps were a thoughtful addition for most users of the trail, but they were nothing more than a series of hurdles for a man dragging his feet with fatigue.

And Scott was *tired*. At the best of times, he slept poorly during his first night on a backpacking trip. The ground was too lumpy, the moon too bright, the sounds of night different than the muffled street noises and muffled groans of refrigerator and heating system that he heard at home. By the second night he was acclimated to the outdoors and slept like a baby.

But that was during normal trips when nobody was trying to kill him. The worries involved in waging a running gun battle with psychopathic arsonists far surpassed the pedestrian concerns about water, food and wildlife that occupied him on his usual jaunts into the desert. He was wiped out; the only thing keeping him going now was his concern for Lani's safety.

He knew he took Lani for granted. Maybe he should think about ... what? Marrying Lani? Well, maybe not *marry* her. They could just shack up together. That would be nice, so long as she didn't hog the bedcovers or give him a hard time about his friends, or his drinking, or the building codes that he wasn't obeying. Not that she was prone to nagging him—her antipathy to any such behavior was a key component to their successful relationship—but his years of hard-won experience cautioned that odd personality changes tended to accompany major shifts in the delicate balance between men and women.

"Maybe I'll just buy her flowers," he grunted.

A bead of sweat dangled from the tip of his nose. It broke away and splashed down on his pumping right knee.

His breath took on a wheezing quality as the trailhead sign crawled slowly into view.

Yeah, flowers. I'll buy Lani flowers and take her out to a nice dinner. And I'll seriously consider the whole shacking-up idea. But not marriage—not yet. I'll hold that off for later.

With his mind racing, Scott dragged himself the last few yards and reached the head of the trail.

"You there."

"Wha—?"

Two men stood by the trailhead. One was tall, older and dressed in a thread-bare sport coat and jeans. A biblical white beard sprouted from his chin. The index finger of his right hand jabbed accusingly at Scott.

"You're not one of my people! And you're not a ranger!" the man said. His voice thundered like he was on stage.

Inhaling sharply, Scott caught his breath.

"Your people? Who in Hell are your—" He stopped. He stared at the man.

The bearded man stared back.

"Oh shit," Scott said.

Chapter 69

Greenfield stared at the stranger in surprise. It wasn't the man's dusty, sweaty appearance that caught his eye—that was standard-issue for anybody enjoying a little time on the trail. Nor was it the somewhat tattered state of his clothing—neither Greenfield nor his companion were fashion plates themselves. No, what grabbed the floral-rights activist's attention was the stranger's look of grim determination.

Well, that and the strange-looking rifle in his hand.

"You're not one of my people!" Greenfield sputtered out of surprise. "And you're not a ranger!"

The man said something back, but the pounding of Greenfield's pulse drowned out everything except one muttered oath.

"Oh shit," Greenfield echoed.

He reached for the gun tucked behind his belt. His hand had just closed around the grip when he realized that he wasn't going to be fast enough. The barrel of the stranger's rifle was already rising.

"Oh shit," Greenfield blurted again. With a sudden surge he charged forward, directly into the stranger. He hit the man before he had a chance to bring the rifle into play. Together, they rolled into the dust, hats and guns scattering where inertia would take them.

Greenfield felt his jaw painfully clamp shut as he hit the ground. He grunted. For long minutes they writhed in the dirt. The stranger was obviously stronger, but desperation allowed the environmental guru to cling tight in a bear hug that pinned one of the man's arms to his side. The free hand pounded like a mallet on Greenfield's head and back, tenderizing flesh wherever it landed.

The men's legs scissored, sending them rolling now into a bush, then over a cactus (ouch). Spines and rocks and branches ripped at skin and tore clothing. A close-up view of the Earth exchanged itself for a cloud-speckled stretch of sky split by a hammer-like fist thundering down on— *Oh.* Greenfield saw stars.

"Do something!" he yelped.

"What do I do?" Happy whined.

"Jump him!"

He felt the stranger's hand closing on his collar and pulling his head off the dirt. He stared up into a cocked fist.

"Jump him now!" His hands batted at the fist without and discernible effect.

"I can't!" Happy's voice climbed frantically in reply.

"Why not?"

"I'm a pacifist!"

"Oh," was all Greenfield had time to say before the fist crashed down. He felt his nose give way and gagged at the sharp pain.

"Good," the stranger said, letting go of Greenfield. His head thumped painfully back to earth. "Then you won't give me any trouble when I pound you."

With his left hand clasped to the pulpy remnants of his proboscis, Greenfield staggered back to his feet. He'd felt his pistol tumble away during the fight, and his pain, watering eyes and simmering panic rendered a search unthinkable.

"Fuck this, he said. Then he turned and bolted toward the

edge of the parking lot and the desert beyond.

From the corner of his eye, he just barely caught a glimpse of Happy's open-mouthed stare. The boy was doubled over, with the stranger's fist stuffed deeply into his belly.

Chapter 70

The McGintys' home was larger than Lani had expected, with an obviously recent addition tacked on to what had once been a modest house on several acres of land. Three vehicles of recent vintage were parked in the gravel driveway. Antennae poked from the roof, aimed alternately at the sky and at nearby Mingus Mountain.

A goat grazed contentedly on a grassy island in the driveway.

"Watch your step, young lady," Bill said, as he helped Lani down from the truck. "We don't want you getting injured now, after what you've already been through."

"Thank you so much."

"Think nothing of it."

"Bill, why don't you show her where the bathroom and the computer are," Emma said. "I'll get her something cold to drink."

Bill nodded.

"Lemonade. From hand-squeezed lemons."

"Oh wow. My favorite."

Lani followed the McGintys through the unlocked front door. Carrying her backpack, Bill turned to the right and she followed. As she did so she caught a brief glimpse of what looked like a large bedroom from the corner of her eye. A reflective silvery screen of the kind she vaguely associated with photography dominated one corner. It seemed an odd décor choice among the Mexican pine furniture.

"Here you go," Bill called from down the hallway. He held a folded towel in one huge hand and waved at a doorway with the other. He'd placed her pack on the floor. "Help yourself to the guest bathroom. I'll get the computer booted up."

Lani took the hint. With a sigh of relief, she helped herself to a large portion of the McGintys' hot water supply and a matching share of soap and shampoo. The shower was refreshing, but she paused before getting dressed. Her clothes were all fairly crusty from days in the desert, but the shirt and shorts she'd worn today were the worst. With a limited selection, it took only a few minutes to pick the outfit that would be the least offensive.

Emma met her in the hallway. Without her cowboy hat her silvery hair made her look grandmotherly. The frosty glass of lemonade in her right hand completed the image.

"Here you go," Emma chirped. "Bill is waiting for you in our office."

"Thanks." She slurped. "This is delicious."

In the office, Bill looked to Lani's eyes like an astronaut, centered as he was in a cockpit-like cocoon of electronic equipment that included no less than three video monitors.

"Oh wow. My boyfriend would really envy your setup here."

"Oh we need it for our business. It's all a big tax write-off," Bill said. "Come over here and take a seat."

Lani pulled up a chair and squeezed into the space next to the big man. She placed the cell phone with its USB cable and the folded paper containing Scott's instructions on the desk in front of her.

"I hope I can download the video from the phone."

Bill chuckled.

"Oh, we can manage if you get stuck." With a quick motion he plugged the cable into the phone and the computer. "There you go."

"Oh. Thanks."

Flattening the sheet of paper with one hand—grains of dirt spilled from its folds onto the wood desktop—Lani began to work. She tapped at the keyboard in hunt-and-peck style, with two fingers curved and jabbing like scorpion stingers. The first task was creating an explanatory email to grab attention and give the video of the arson some context. She and Scott—assisted by Rollo's inflammatory recommendations—had spent plenty of time talking over the particulars of the text, and she had a rough draft written down. The email would link to the video.

Next, she had to upload the video to Scott's YouTube account. That went without a hitch.

The last task was to send the letter she'd written to the distribution list Scott's old company used for media contacts.

"Shit."

"What is it?" Bill asked.

"Oh. I'm sorry about my language."

"This house has heard worse. Let's see ..."

Bill leaned in to peer at the screen.

"It's not taking your password."

"No. They must have changed the password after they fired Scott. I don't know what to do next."

Bill tugged at the brim of the hat perched on his head.

"Well, what are you trying to accomplish?"

"I'm trying to send the video to Scott's old media-contact list. It's full of tech journalists who might be able to help us. But it's not letting me do it."

"So, you just need to get that video out to as many important eyeballs as possible?"

"Yes. The more people who see the video, the less reason the people chasing us will have to hurt us. It won't do them any good if the video is all over the Internet. But now I'm stuck."

Emma's hand came down on Lani's shoulder.

"Bill. Let's let her use our distribution list. It's full of politicians and press people."

Lani looked up at her hosts.

"Really? Out of curiosity. What kind of business do you have?"

Bill chuckled.

"Adult entertainment over the Internet. You know, porn. It's a goldmine."

Emma patted Lani's shoulder.

"You wouldn't believe who's on our list."

Chapter 71

Scott turned as a flash of movement caught his eye. He saw a dirty, tattered figure flee into the desert.

"Hey!"

The man bobbed and weaved, as if dodging gunfire. He took no notice of Scott's call and made quick progress through the brush, leaving a plume of dust tossed up by his pounding feet.

Scott turned from the squatting, retching figure in front of him and took a few half-hearted steps in pursuit. He never got beyond a jog, and then froze in place, agonizing over his next move. He began to reach for his rifle, and then dismissed the thought of shooting at a fleeing man.

"Goddamn it."

He realized he'd made a tactical error. By attempting to subdue both of the men, he'd let one escape. And now he had no time to go chasing off into the desert when Lani might well need his help.

Scott turned back to the pathetic figure on the ground. He stretched his foot out to prod the man, but he elicited a whimper before his toe ever made contact.

"Don't hurt me!"

"I already did that. Answer my questions and I won't hurt

you *again*."

No answer.

Scott stretched out his foot.

"OK! OK!"

"Who is that crazy old bastard who went charging off into the desert?

"You mean Dr. Greenfield?"

Scott squinted. The name rang a bell. Yep—it had featured prominently during the nighttime interrogation session he and Rollo had conducted with that wounded fed wannabe. Fuck. He had screwed up even worse than he thought.

"He's that tree-power nut, right?"

Still obviously in pain, the man managed to look indignant.

"He runs the Center for Floral Supremacy! He's a visionary."

"Uh huh. He's a real leader. He left your sorry ass to bleed while he hightailed it into the desert."

Indignation turned to mournfulness. This time, Scott had to actually make contact with his toe to get a reaction.

"On your way in here, did you see a woman—a blonde?" Scott helpfully held his hand about Lani's height off the ground. "About this tall—"

Vigorous headshaking. "No. We just got here. You're the first person we saw."

Frustrated and worried, Scott spared a last glance in the direction Greenfield had disappeared. Then he looked down at the remaining floral-supremacist.

"Give me your wallet."

"Why?"

Sharp jab with a toe.

"Ow! All right!"

Scott grabbed the proffered bright-red nylon monstrosity and yanked the driver's license from its protective pocket.

"This your current address, Henry?"

Happy nodded before catching himself. His eyes widened.

"Good."

The wallet landed on not-so-Happy's chest.

"Don't wander too far," Scott said. "I'd hate to have to hunt you down.

Then he started walking down the road.

Chapter 72

"Ummm ... Really?"

"Oh, yes." Bill said. "It's not easy to make a living around here. There's the cement plant, the hospital, the usual small businesses ..."

He shrugged.

"But then the Internet came along and made it possible to sell anything to anybody anywhere. And what's easier to sell than what comes naturally?

At a loss for anything else to say, Lani managed a noncommittal "oh" as she glanced back and forth between the ... umm ... generously proportioned McGintys.

They caught her look.

"Oh!" Emma started. "Not us." She sighed. "You'd think more people would appreciate us full-figured folks. No, we hire people who do the honors, record the action and distribute it online."

She pursed her lips.

"In fact, you clean up really–"

"Nope!" Lani yelped. "Thanks, but no thanks."

"Suit yourself! There's good money in it."

Bill cleared his throat.

"Maybe this is a conversation to save for later, dear."

Emma fluttered her hands.

"You're right! I'm sorry, sweety. You have plenty enough on your mind. Now, why don't we get that video of yours onto our servers."

"It's already up on YouTube."

"Oh, YouTube will fold the first time somebody official waves a take-down order at them, and we already know you're dealing with government people. Our servers are in Amsterdam. And so is the company that officially owns them. I think we can keep your video online a good long time, even *after* they find a lawyer who speaks Dutch."

"Really?"

"Yep. This isn't our first legal rodeo."

Lani nodded. "Cool."

"Is your email ready to go?"

"Yes."

"Paste it in here."

Bill reached over Lani and tapped briefly at the keyboard.

"What now?"

"Well …" Emma said. "I suspect you've just caused a … well … a bit of a shit-storm, dear. Glad we could help!"

"That's … great." She paused. "Scott and Rollo are still in trouble. I need to get back to them. Could I borrow some ammunition?"

"I don't see why not. If you don't mind, we'll tag along and make it a party. We'd planned a hike, anyway."

Chapter 73

S cott wasn't often at a loss for something to do, but now was an exceptional moment. Oh sure, he could *walk*. In fact, he *was* walking. And he had a lot of walking ahead of him, considering the length of the road to town. Clarkdale, wasn't it? It was ten miles, more or less, if he remembered right. He wasn't sure he did, when it came down to it.

But that was it. He couldn't call anybody, because Lani had his phone. He couldn't flag anybody down because nobody had come along since he began his walk. And he couldn't ...

Hello. What in Hell was that?

Along the side of the road, in a ditch, was a wrecked Park Service SUV. The windshield was smashed, as was the driver's-side window. A deep dent marred the hood. Square-ish shards of safety glass littered the ground around the vehicle, scattered around an abandoned lug wrench.

With a shrug, Scott walked over for a closer look.

Blood speckled the door handle and a peek inside revealed a brownish-red smear on the steering wheel. Interestingly, the key dangled from the steering column.

Carefully, he eased into the driver's seat, brushing away glass as he did so. He held his breath as he gave the key a twist, then exhaled explosively when nothing happened.

"No, that would have been too much to hope for."

He noticed rust-colored flecks on his fingers when he released the key. They spotted his fingers like snowflakes from Hell. He recognized them as yet another sample of dried blood.

With a flash of belated insight, he thought back to the dead ranger in Sycamore Canyon. Now he understood why the man had looked so thoroughly mauled even before stopping Lani's bullet.

"Jesus Christ," Scott muttered. "It's almost a waste of effort to fight these people. They beat the crap out of themselves."

Back out on the road, Scott resignedly set one foot in front of the other and resumed his trek toward town. He had begun working up another sweat when he noticed a plume of dust headed his way on the road.

Typical. Traffic at last, but headed in the wrong direction.

As the vehicle neared, Scott stepped to the side to put himself out of harm's way. You never knew about some of these cowboys, who could make a half-ton truck skid along a dirt road with all of the grace of a toboggan on black ice. He then waved his arms over his head with the vague thought of borrowing a cell phone to call Lani. He could even pay for the favor, if it came to that. He was certainly *going* to be broke, unless he found a new job soon, but there were still a few greenbacks crowding his wallet.

Much to his surprise, the arm-waving worked. At least, the dust cloud stopped moving and settled around him, amidst much screeching of brakes.

And a familiar voice.

"Hey, baby! Going our way?"

The dust settled, and he noticed the expected pickup truck, with a horse trailer attached behind, and Lani leaning out the rear window of the truck's extended cab.

"These are our new friends, Bill and Emma."

A bit thrown, Scott just waved.

"They have horses and guns and other friends on the way."

Scott nodded, impressed. It seemed like the right thing to do, to acknowledge people he'd never met who were willing to bear arms against deranged, half-naked, government-employed arsonists.

A large woman leaned out the shotgun window.

"Well, get in, son!"

Scott took the hint, legging his way up through the open door and into the rear seat next to Lani.

"Honey," he said, "Are you all right? I found Champ's grave and ... uh ..."

"The ranger's body, too?" Lani asked.

Scott nodded his head, while glancing at the driver.

"Yeah, they know. I had to do it, honey. He would have killed me if Champ hadn't jumped in."

"He was a good dog."

Lani sniffed and wiped at her eye with the sleeve of her shirt.

"The best."

Scott looked to his new allies.

"So, you folks are OK ..."

"We are."

"Yup!"

"Lani showed us the video and made us into true believers."

Emma chuckled.

"Not that we would have needed much convincing. We've had our own run-ins with jacked-up authority types."

Scott glanced at Lani.

"They make porn."

Scott was generally a pretty good card player, but there are times when even the best poker face crumbles.

"I'll explain later," she added.

"It's all good by me," Scott said. "I'm always happy to make new friends."

"Us, too," Bill said, shooting a quick smile over the seat before returning his attention to the road. "That's a tough little lady you have there."

"Apparently tougher than I ever knew. Which reminds me … If you see a scrawny redhead or an old buzzard in a rancid-looking sport coat, could you stop?"

"Sure," Bill answered. "Why?"

"They're bad guys, and they need another punch in the head."

Chapter 74

Rollo couldn't have been happier to see his friends. It wasn't loneliness so much—in fact, he'd had plenty of company. But the awareness that his company was murderously inclined toward him soured the social aspect of his situation. And that sourness was amplified by the knowledge that he was feeling a tad drowsy, and that if he succumbed to the temptation to shut his eyes for a moment, those murderous companions were likely to dismantle him in no time flat.

So when Lani and Scott came into view like the proverbial cavalry. Proverbial, Hell! They were mounted on horseback like the *real* cavalry, even if Scott appeared to be stoically suffering from a brewing case of hemorrhoids. And they weren't alone; right alongside them rode a half-dozen obvious civilians, all festooned with a variety of devices designed to put holes great and small in objects at a distance. They were clearly on friendly terms with their companions, and Rollo happily took them at face value as allies when he rose to wave a greeting.

"Hey, there!" he yelled, waving his hat with one hand, gripping his rifle with the other, and bracing his feet in a successful effort to avoid the siren call of gravity. "Glad you brought friends!"

"Cops are probably right behind us," Scott yelled back.

"Sheriff's deputies were pulling up as we hit the trail."

Rollo grunted, taking the information as it was likely intended—as a heads-up. He slung his ancient British rifle over his shoulder and began climbing down.

"Cops!" somebody shouted. Rollo was pretty sure it was the mouthier of the male firebugs—the one with the bandaged shoulder. What was his name? Bob ... Yeah, Bob. He stood next to the quiet, skinny guy who always looked a bit confused. "About time! You guys are dead."

"Not as dead ... ugh ... Not as dead as the prick you sent to cut us off at the trailhead."

That was Scott, dismounting from his borrowed horse with a minimum of grace. Well ... So there *was* an outdoorsy thing at which Scott sucked! Not that Rollo would get much mileage from the knowledge—he hadn't been on horseback since summer camp as a kid.

Damn, he'd hated summer camp All of those rules ...

"Wait," Rollo said, Scott's comment belatedly registering. He jumped the last couple of feet to the canyon floor. "You shot one of the fuckers?"

Scott stood in obvious discomfort, very obviously trying not to rub parts of his anatomy that ought not be handled in public.

"No. Lani did. After he killed Champ."

Dismounted herself, with a bit more grace than her boyfriend, Lani nodded a silent confirmation and turned her eyes away.

"Awww, shit." Rollo turned to glare at the firebugs. "I liked that dog."

Open-mouthed and quiet through the brief discussion, Bob started jabbering.

"You killed Tim?" He glanced back and forth between Scott and Lani.

"That bitch killed Tim?" That was the woman shaped like a fire hydrant. She'd jumped up from her apparently permanent station by the injured guy Rollo and Scott had questioned to take an aggressive stance next to Bob.

"Shut up, assholes." Rollo snarled. "There's no reason we have to stop there."

He joined Lani and Scott.

"So," he said. "Apparently the dead prick's name was 'Tim'."

Lani didn't seem all that interested in the news.

"This is going to be tough for the cops to get past, isn't it?" she asked. "Even though I was defending myself, they'll just back up the guy in the uniform."

Scott didn't answer, but simply put his arms around her.

Rollo grimaced, then strolled over to introduce himself to the new arrivals.

Chapter 75

So far as Scott could tell, he and his friends had done everything possible to survive a shitty situation. But Lani was right. He'd never once heard of cops getting chummy with people who'd exchanged gunfire with their buddies. He was pretty sure that even the traditional rivalry between feds and local officials wasn't going to be enough to overcome the us-against-the-world code of law-enforcement officers.

And so he just held Lani and hoped that the video they'd sent out brewed up a helpful shitstorm before he and his friends had been too thoroughly run through the jailhouse meat grinder.

A few feet away, Bill called to Rollo.

"Is that all of them?"

Rollo glanced at the prisoners, then snorted.

"Hey asshole," he yelled to Bob. "Where are the other two? The hippie chick and your fearless leader?"

Bob shrugged and looked away.

Emma put her hand on Scott's shoulder.

"We have this," she said.

With mild interest, Scott watched as Bill, Emma and another of the new arrivals went in search of the missing firebugs. The others stayed to guard the prisoners.

The sight of Rollo stooping to briefly paw through a backpack near the man Scott had shot in the ass briefly stirred his curiosity. The man on the ground never moved, lying still with his arm over his eyes. He seemed totally uninterested in events around him.

Before he could begin to speculate about Rollo's actions, however, a roar overhead caught his attention.

"Oh, we have company," he said to Lani.

Bursting into view over the canyon wall came a low-flying helicopter. It overshot the group, circled back, and then hovered in place.

"That has to be from the sheriff's department. Probably making sure it's safe for the deputies to come in."

Half-heartedly, Scott waved at the chopper.

"Hey there!"

Surprised by the loud hail, Scott turned to see Rollo waving with unexpected enthusiasm. His rifle was clenched in one hand.

"Small suggestion, buddy," Scott called out. "Don't wave the gun at the cops."

"Oh shit!" Rollo dropped the rifle to the ground, then resumed his vigorous waving.

The chopper dipped in seeming acknowledgment, then roared away.

Scott took a deep breath, bracing himself for the new arrivals. From the corner of his eye he saw movement, and turned to find Bill and Emma leading the missing couple back to the group. Even under an impressive layer of grime, the two seemed to be ... blushing.

"This is great!" Bill enthused. He waved his smart phone over his head. "You wouldn't believe what these two were up to. I recorded it all!" He turned to the strays. "You guys have talent."

The pair actually seemed to turn crimson.

"What in Hell … ?," Scott asked.

"I'm not sure what to call it," Bill answered. "Maybe nature porn—"

"Erotica, dear," Emma interrupted. She gently placed her hand on her husband's arm. "Eco-erotica."

As Lani rested her head against his chest and quietly giggled, Scott just shook his head.

Chapter 76

Jason wasn't sure just how things had gone so horribly, horribly wrong. Well, so horribly, horribly wrong *again*.

It wasn't so much being interrupted while mid- ... well ... thrust with Samantha by that odd redneck couple. Yes, that was humiliating, but, frankly, he was fairly accustomed to humiliation by now. It was almost an old friend.

No, it was the *frustration*. After all, when the sheriff's deputies arrived, the snoops they'd been chasing were all immediately lined up facing the canyon wall. And their redneck friends were disarmed by the cops and told to keep their mouths shut. After a cold, thirsty and frightening Hell of hiking and shooting through Sycamore Canyon, Jason seemed close to accomplishing his mission and protecting his crusade or Carthage Option or ... well, he'd have to think about it. And he'd been within reach of victory all because that meathead Tim had finally done the right thing. He'd got himself shot.

The cops really hadn't liked that. They'd been awfully solicitous of Jason and his team, commiserating over their fallen comrade further down the canyon, and applying a slightly higher degree of medical care than Rena had managed to Ray's wounded posterior and Bob's shoulder.

It was all going so well.

And then …

One of the deputies—the one who *didn't* have a soup-strainer mustache—straightened up from where he was kneeling by Ray. The ranger's backpack lay unzipped and open at his feet. His eyes were unreadable behind his aviator shades, but the item in his hand said all that needed to be said.

It was a bag. Suspended between two gloved fingers, it was a freezer bag, transparent—well, trans*lucent* beneath a coating of dirt—and filled with a large quantity of dried vegetable matter.

"We have something here."

Ray managed to prop himself up on one arm and gawk—just before the deputy planted a foot in his chest and pressed him back to the ground.

Another deputy promptly snatched a candy bar back from Terry.

Well … If there's anything that cops like less than cop-killers, it's even a hint that somebody doesn't take the drug laws completely seriously.

Why did dumb-ass Ray haul dope on the mission?

And, if he was going to bring it, why didn't he share?

Damn, those handcuffs hurt.

Chapter 77

"The head is too square," Lani protested. She moved around for a better view, then peered at an angle. "Well, it's a *little* too square."

"Face it, honey," Scott answered. "He had a square head."

"Like a fucking brick," Rollo chimed in.

The three of them stood in the packed-dirt parking lot at the trailhead into Sycamore Canyon. Lani wore a green dress that was, perhaps, just a little light for the chilly, overcast day. She kept her arms folded in a gesture that gave off less of an air of displeasure than of a need to conserve body temperature. Scott was better prepared for the weather in a tweed jacket, tie and corduroy trousers. Rollo had impressed just by showing up in something reasonably clean.

Lani and Scott studiously refrained from commenting on the glasses perched on their friend's nose—a heroic effort, considering their sturdy frames and the frequency with which he fussed with them.

"He was a good dog," Lani insisted.

"No disagreement here," Scott said. He took off his jacket and draped it over Lani's shoulders. "He was the best."

Rollo grunted assent and bent down for a closer look at the

object of their scrutiny.

Rendered in bronze by an artist friend of Lani and Scott, within feet of the trailhead itself, was a sculpture of Champ. Lifelike, even if his head was a bit more square than Lani liked, bronze Champ grinned and had his leg raised to pee on an equally metallic ranger hat.

The money for the sculpture had been raised by private subscription. The Forest Service consented to its placement, and even sent an official to attend the unveiling, only under the duress resulting from the significant public good will enjoyed by Scott, Lani and Rollo after their misadventure.

Which is to say, the dust of the official's exit from the unveiling party was still settling over the assembled attendees.

That duress hadn't been hard to come by. The shit storm that Scott had so fervently wished for that day in Sycamore Canyon, many months earlier, had quickly brewed.

And events ... well ... events were moving along in sometimes strange ways.

"Hey Lani! Guys!"

The trio turned to greet Bill and Emma.

"So ... " Bill tried—unsuccessfully—to suppress a smirk. "I just want to thank you folks for sparing us from a dastardly drug conspiracy."

Emma jabbed him in the ribs.

"That's not funny, dear. Not everybody appreciates your sense of humor."

Scott smiled and shrugged.

"That's what the feds have decided. And who are we to contradict them? Especially with the potential for some very interesting felony charges hanging over our heads if we object to our new status as heroes against ... *sigh* ... narco-terrorism."

Bill nodded.

"Yeah. I'm sorry about that. Speaking of felony charges ... That Ray fellow—the one you tagged in the butt—looks to be facing the most time in prison. Because of the dope they found on him, they've tapped him and the dead guy as some sort of drug kingpins in charge of a marijuana-growing operation."

Rollo suddenly began staring at the clouds.

"The feds insist he planned on burning down Williams and Flagstaff, maybe to make room for a huge marijuana plantation," Bill continued. "They aren't too clear on that point."

"Doesn't matter if it's clear or even if it makes sense," Scott said. "It'll be a long time before he sees the light of day again."

"The only person sticking by him is that stocky girl," Emma chimed in. "I don't remember her name."

Scott snorted as he recalled Rena.

"She's facing charges herself, though, and I don't think her talk of a mammalian conspiracy is doing him any good."

He grimaced.

"Not that I give a damn. After what we went through, anything—" He placed his hand on Rollo's shoulder and looked around to make sure none of the other scattered unveiling attendees were too close. "Anything that puts them away is fine by me. Even really smelly ditch weed planted in a psycho's backpack by my buddy in a burst of inspiration."

"It wasn't ditch weed," Rollo protested. "It was just old."

"It stank."

Rollo rolled his eyes.

Bill sighed.

"Yeah, but we could use that weird little tree-hugger couple. That video we took went viral." He put his arm around Emma. "I am so glad that my better half always carries a couple of release forms with her. When those two get out, they'll have some money waiting for them."

Emma smiled.

"We've build a whole new Website around eco-erotica. It's doing very well." She glanced at Lani and Scott. "We're always looking for new performers."

"I'm very happy for you," Lani said, a bit abruptly. "Good luck with that!"

"Maybe if I lost some weight...?," Rollo ventured.

Bill just shook his head.

"Of course," said Rollo, returning to the main topic. "We never touched the bigwigs."

"That floral supremacy freak is still on the loose," said Lani.

Scott shrugged.

"The last I saw of him, he was racing into the desert as fast as his legs could take him. But I suppose he had to stop some time. And I doubt he's any less crazy for the experience."

"Nope," added Scott. "And that Forest Service guy Ray told us about ... Van Kamp? He's doing just fine as head of the investigation into the drug plot." He made scare quotes in the air with his fingers at the mention of the supposed narcotics conspiracy.

"Let's not forget," answered Bill. "He's bringing in experts from the timber industry to help manage the public lands while he gets to the bottom of the drug plot." He slapped his thigh. "You know somebody is making a killing on *that* little scam."

Lani grabbed Scott's right arm and raised it in the air.

"Honey ..." Scott cautioned.

"Oh, tell them," she chirped, releasing his arm.

Scott shrugged.

"I sort of figured the feds would find a way to grease their buddies' palms, and their own, with this situation. Why let a serious crisis go to waste, right? So I took a chance and put my remaining money into stocks." He spread his hands. "I figured it would be either mining or timber. I bet on timber."

Emma chuckled and shook her head.

"Hey, if I'm going to be screwed, I want to get paid."

"You know we don't disagree, son," said Bill.

There was silence for a long moment. Then Rollo leaned forward.

"Remember that day we met?"

Scott nodded.

"We have a lot more tires to slash."

Chapter 78

In the grass, not too far from the trailhead, Rupert Greenfield lay prone, watching the proceedings through his binoculars and grinding his teeth in a rhythmic motion.

"Dog lovers!," he snarled. "I *hate* dog lovers."

He turned to his companion, sprawled near him and poking listlessly in the dirt.

"We're not done, you know. The plants still need us. We have a lot of work to do."

"I know."

Greenfield returned to peering through his binoculars. His jaws continued to work.

"We need to gather more of the old crew. You get on that."

"OK."

"And, Happy, I need more supplies. I'm running out of everything out here."

"Henry."

"What?"

"Not Happy. Just Henry."

"Whatever. Just make sure you get me a hat and some jerky."

About the Author

J.D. Tuccille's provocative and often witty columns on hotly debated topics including the environment, land use and forest management have appeared in publications including the *Arizona Republic*, the *Denver Post*, the *Providence Journal* and the *Washington Times*. The former editor of a popular civil liberties website, Tuccille has commented on current issues on both television and radio, and has been quoted saying unkind things about politicians and government policies in the pages of the *New York Times*, *Salon* and other publications.

Tuccille is an enthusiastic explorer of the American Southwest's deserts, mountains and forests. He lives in rural northern Arizona with his wife, Wendy, a pediatrician, their son, Anthony, and their two dogs.

Did you enjoy reading *High Desert Barbecue*? You can purchase more copies of this book in trade paperback and Kindle versions at Amazon.com, and for the Nook at BarnesandNoble.com.

Follow news about *High Desert Barbecue* at:
http://www.facebook.com/pages/High-Desert-Barbecue/261709117207918

Made in the USA
Middletown, DE
25 June 2015